DRAMOCLES

BOOKS BY ROBERT SHECKLEY

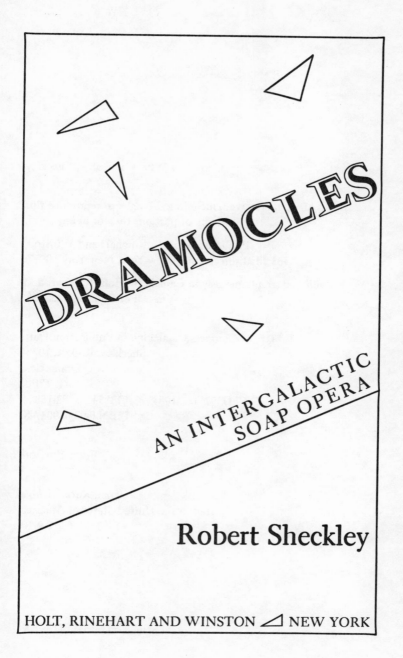

DRAMOCLES

AN INTERGALACTIC SOAP OPERA

Robert Sheckley

HOLT, RINEHART AND WINSTON ◁ NEW YORK

Published by Holt, Rinehart and Winston,
383 Madison Avenue, New York, New York 10017.

Published simultaneously in Canada by Holt, Rinehart and
Winston of Canada, Limited.

Library of Congress Cataloging in Publication Data
Sheckley, Robert, 1928-
Dramocles.
I. Title.
PS3569.H392D7   1983   813'.54   82-15864
ISBN 0-03-059037-X

First Edition

Designer: *Kate Nichols*
Printed in the United States of America
1 2 3 4 5 6 7 8 9 10

ISBN 0-03-059037-X

To Jay, with Love

DRAMOCLES

1

King Dramocles, ruler of Glorm, awoke and looked about him and couldn't remember where he was. This happened to him frequently because of his habit of sleeping in different rooms in his palace as the mood struck him. His palace of Ultragnolle was the largest man-made structure on Glorm, and perhaps in the galaxy. It was so large that it required its own internal transportation system. Within this colossal structure, Dramocles had forty-seven personal bedrooms. He also kept another sixty or so rooms equipped with couches, pullout beds, convertible sofas, air mattresses, and the like, for impulse sleeping. On account of this, going to bed was a nightly adventure for him, and waking up was a daily mystery.

Sitting up and looking around, Dramocles discovered that he had spent the night sleeping on a pile of cushions in one of the Hirsute Rooms, so called because of the large clumps of black hair growing in the corners.

With that much settled, he turned to the matter of coffee.

Generally, this involved no more than pressing a button beside the bed. This would sound an alarm in the royal kitchen, activating the enormous cappuccino machine. It had a boiler large enough to drive a locomotive, and ten servants worked around the clock stoking the fires beneath it, cleaning filters, adding freshly ground coffee, and performing all of the other steps. Shortly thereafter, steamed cappuccino, exactly sugared to the king's taste, was supposed to flow through miles of copper tubing, coming out at last through a spigot in whatever room Dramocles desired to have it in.

This time, however, Dramocles had slept in a part of the palace that was not yet plugged into the coffee circuit. Grumpily he slipped on a pair of jeans and a T-shirt and went out into the corridor.

A neatly stenciled sign on the corridor wall told him that he was at coordinates R52-J26. A monorail ran down the middle of the corridor, so at least he was within the palace transportation network. Of course, there was no train in sight. Dramocles consulted the schedule posted on the wall, and saw that the next train—a Cross Palace Local—was not due for another forty minutes. He lifted the emergency phone from the wall and called Transport Central.

The telephone rang many times. At last an uncultured voice said, "Yeah, whaddya want?"

"I want a train sent to me immediately," Dramocles said.

"You do, hah? Well, forget it, buddy. Half our trains are in the repair shop and the rest of them are at locations of more importance than where you're at.

2

There's nothing out where you're at except a lot of hairy bedrooms."

"This is King Dramocles speaking," Dramocles said, in a dangerous voice.

"For real? Let me just check your voice print. . . . Yeah, you really are. Hey, Sire, I'm sorry about how I talked to you, but you know how it is, noblemen calling me at all hours of the day or night trying to get trains diverted for their personal convenience. Especially now, because of the peace celebrations."

"Never mind," Dramocles said. "How soon can you get a train to me?"

"Seven minutes, Sire. I'll divert the Pantheon Express just before it pulls into Chapultepec Station, and—"

"Does it have coffee-making equipment aboard?"

"I'll just check that. . . . No, Sire, the Pantheon only carries instant coffee and stale Danish. Give me twenty minutes and I can get you a modern breakfast train—"

"Just send what's nearest," Dramocles said. "I'll have my breakfast later."

Fifteen minutes passed. No train came down the monorail. Dramocles picked up the telephone again, but all he could get was a maddening series of clicks. At last a recorded voice told him that all circuits were busy and he would have to place his call through the palace operator. In vain Dramocles shouted that *he* was the King and that all other calls should be disconnected at once. No one was listening.

He stalked back to his bedroom to get his cigarettes, but now he couldn't find which room he had slept in. All of the rooms in this sector were hirsute. Nor did any of the other telephones seem to work. Not even the fire alarm gave any response.

Furious, Dramocles stomped down the corridor. He figured he had at least an hour's hike before he reached one of the populated sectors of Ultragnolle. What had he been doing out here in this godforsaken sector last night? He seemed to remember a party, some drugs, some booze, a lot of laughter, and then, oblivion. He trudged along and stopped when he heard the sound of a motor behind him.

Far down the corridor he could see something tiny with a winking yellow light coming toward him. It grew in size, and was discernible at last as a corridor car, a type of one-wheeled vehicle used by the nobility to get around the palace in a hurry.

The car came to a neat stop beside him. The bubble top opened and a cheerful, curly-haired boy of twelve or so looked out and said, "Is that you, Father?"

"Of course it's me," Dramocles said. "Which one are you?"

"I'm Samizat, Father," the boy said. "My mother is Andrea, whom you divorced two years ago."

"Andrea? Small, dark-haired woman with a piercing voice?"

"That's her. We live in the St. Michel sector of Glorm. Mother frequently telephones you about her dreams."

"Portents she calls them," Dramocles said. He got in beside Samizat. "Take me to Palace Central." Samizat threw the corridor car into gear and accelerated fast enough to scorch the wax on the corridor floor.

After a while the corridor opened into a wide, balustraded balcony. Samizat turned abruptly down a long flight of stairs, then slowed as they approached the vast domed room that contained St. Leopold's Square. It was an important regional market, filled with striped tents in front of which men and aliens sat and sold a great variety of goods. There were Geiselmen from Glorm's northernmost province, offering bright wallisberries in small wicker baskets. There were Grots, members of the ancient race that had inhabited Glorm before the arrival of humans, nodding over their bowls of narcotic porridge. Brungers from Dispasia and the flatlands of Arnapest were there too, imposing in their national costume of polished leather and taffeta, offering the intricately carved walking sticks and miniature peaches for which they were famous. And, floating high above the animated scene, were the great blue and gold banners that proclaimed this the thirtieth year of the Pax Glormicae.

Dramocles spotted a coffeehouse and had his son drop him there. He gulped a double cappuccino, signed for it, and took a corridor taxi to Palace Central.

Rudolphus, the Chamberlain, was waiting for him by the inner steps, agitation showing on his plump, mustached face.

"Sire," he said, "you are late for the audience!"

"Since I am the King," Dramocles said, "I can't be late because whenever I get here is the right time."

"Casuistry aside," Rudolphus said, "you set the time for the audience yourself, and you ordered me to scold you if you were late."

"Consider me scolded. Tonight is the official beginning of the Pax Glormicae celebration, I believe?"

5

"It is, Sire, and everything is in readiness. King Adalbert of Aardvark arrived last night, and we housed him in the small mansion on the rue Mountjoy. Lord Rufus of Druth is here with his retinue, and they have been given Trontium Castle for their stay. King Snint of Lekk is in the Rose Garden Hotel on Temple Avenue. Your brother, Count John of Crimsole, is docking in the spaceport even now. Only King Haldemar of Vanir has neglected to show up or even RSVP."

"Just as we suspected. I will meet with the kings later. Was there anything interesting in today's mail?"

"Just the usual junk."

Rudolphus gave Dramocles a bunch of letters, which Dramocles shoved into a hip pocket. "I'll get to this later. Now, let's have that audience. And try to move it along faster this time, Rudolphus."

"Sire, unless you order otherwise, I will follow the protocol exactly as it was laid down by your revered father, Otho the Weird."

Dramocles shrugged. Otho's rules, laws, and precepts were for the most part highly useful, and Dramocles had never gotten around to thinking of rules to replace them with. He entered the audience chamber, followed closely by Rudolphus.

◢ 2

The audience was the usual boring affair of deciding the penalties for various counts and barons who had come under the royal disfavor for cheating the peasants, or the tax machines, or each other. There wasn't anything for Dramocles to do, or even to think about, because the Chamberlain had already made all of the decisions, following the precepts of Otho the Weird. The cases droned on, and Dramocles sat on the high throne and felt sorry for himself.

Despite being absolute monarch of Glorm, and preeminent throughout the Local Planets, Dramocles knew that he had done very little with his life, had just responded to circumstances and absentmindedly ruled Glorm through a long period of unprecedented peace. Bored and unhappy, he fidgeted on his throne and chain-smoked and thought to himself that being a great king was not so great after all. And then the old woman stepped forward, and from that moment everything in his life changed.

She was a small, humpbacked old woman dressed entirely in black except for her gray shoes and wimple. She pressed through the crowd of lesser nobility and made as to approach the throne, until the guards stopped her with their crossed halberds. Then she called out, "O great King!"

"Yes, old lady," said Dramocles, motioning the outraged Rudolphus to be quiet. "I take it you wish to address us. Please do so, and for your sake I hope it's good."

"Sire," she said, "I must humbly request private audience. What I am to say is solely for the ear of the King."

"Indeed?" Dramocles said.

"Aye, indeed," the old woman replied.

Dramocles looked at her appraisingly, and a change so subtle as to be unnoticeable crossed his high-colored features. He snubbed his cigarette in an ashtray carved from a single emerald.

"Lead her to the Green Chamber," he said to the nearest guard. "There she may await our pleasure. Will that suit you, my dear?"

"Yes, Sire, so long as it is not orange."

The court gasped at her effrontery. But Dramocles merely smiled and, after the guard had led the woman away, signaled the Chamberlain to get on with the day's business.

An hour later the audience had ended for the day. Dramocles went to the Green Chamber. There he seated himself in a comfortable armchair, lit up a cigarette, and turned to the old lady who sat primly before him in a straight-backed chair.

"So," he said, "you have come."

"At the very time appointed," the old woman said. "It took no little courage for me to bring myself to your awesome presence, and I did so only because I greatlier feared the not doing so."

"At first I thought you were a crazy person," Dramocles said. "But then I said to you, 'Indeed,' and you replied, 'Aye, indeed,' and I recognized one of the mnemonics that I use as a private recognition code between me and my agents. In the next sentence I used the

8

word *green,* and you replied with *orange,* putting the matter beyond doubt. Did I teach you others?"

"Ten others, making twelve in all, so that I could signal to you somehow if a different sequentiation of dialogue had occurred between us."

"Twelve mnemonics," Dramocles marveled. "My entire stock! I must have judged this a matter of earth-shaking importance. I don't even know your name, old woman."

"That, Sire, is how you said it would be, back when you taught me the mnemonics. My name is Clara."

"A mystery! And it's happening to me!" Dramocles said happily. "Tell your story, Clara."

Clara said, "O great King, you visited me thirty years ago, in my city of Murl, where I earned a modest living remembering things for people who are too busy to remember them for themselves. You said to me, 'Clara' (reading my name above the door—Clara's Rememberatorium), 'I have a message of great importance that I want you to learn by heart and tell me thirty years from today, when I shall need to remember it. I myself will not even remember this conversation until you come to remind me of it, because that's the way it's got to be.'

" 'You may rely on me, Highness,' I said.

" 'Of that I have no doubt,' you replied, 'because I have taken the precaution of putting your name on the official criminal calendar, to be executed summarily thirty years and one day from today. That way, I figure you're going to show up on time.' And then you smiled at me, Sire, gave me the message, and took your departure."

"You must have been a trifle nervous about possible unexpected delays on your way here," Dramocles said.

"I took the precaution of moving to your great city

9

of Ultragnolle shortly after our meeting, and setting up my trade of Remembrancer in the Street of the Armorers just five minutes' walk from the palace."

"You are a wise and prudent woman, Clara. Now, tell me what I told you to tell me."

"Very well, Sire. The key word is—Shazaam!"

Upon hearing that word from the Ancient Tongue, Dramocles was flooded with a luminous memory of a certain day thirty years past.

◁3

Thirty years sped backward like a dissolving newsreel montage. Young Dramocles, twenty years old, sat in his private study, sobbing. He had just received the news that his father, King Otho of Glorm, popularly called "The Weird," had died minutes ago when his laboratory on the moonlet Gliese had blown up. Presumably this was due to some miscalculation on Otho's part, since he was the only person in the laboratory or even on Gliese at the time. It was a fittingly flamboyant way for the king to depart, in an atomic explosion that had blown apart the entire moonlet.

Tomorrow, all Glorm would be in mourning. Later in the week, a coronation would be held, confirming Dramocles as the new king. Although he looked forward to this, Dramocles cried because he had loved his difficult and unpredictable father. But grief struggled with joy in his heart, because, just before his ill-fated trip to Gliese, Otho had had a heart-to-heart talk with his son, reminding him of his duties and responsibilities when he was king, and then quite unexpectedly revealing to him the great destiny that Dramocles had before him.

Dramocles had been amazed by what Otho had told him. He had always wanted a destiny. Now his life would have meaning and purpose, and those were the greatest things anyone could have.

There was only one hitch. As Otho had explained, Dramocles could not begin the active pursuit of his destiny just yet. He was going to have to wait, and it would be a long wait. Thirty years would have to pass before the conditions were right. Only then could the work of Dramocles' destiny begin, and not a day sooner.

Thirty years! A lifetime! And not only was he going to have to wait, he was also going to have to keep his destiny a secret until the moment for action came. There was nobody he could trust with something as big as this. No one must know, not even his most trusted friends and advisers.

"Damn it all," Dramocles grumbled, "come to think of it, I can't even trust myself with this. I'll just blurt it out sometime when I'm stoned or tripping or drunk. I'm the last person I'd trust with a secret like this."

He brooded for a while, chain-smoking cigarettes and considering various alternatives. At last he came to a momentous decision and called for his psychiatric android, Dr. Fish.

"Fish," he said briskly, "I have a certain train of thought in my mind. I don't want to remember it."

"Easy enough to suppress a thought, or even an entire topic," Fish said, in the squeaky voice that androids have despite great advances in voicebox technology. "Your esteemed father, Otho, always had me blot out the names of mistresses who didn't work out, all except their birthdays, since he was a kindly man. He also insisted upon not remembering the color blue."

"But I don't want to lose this thought, either," Dramocles said. "It's a very important thought. I want to remember it thirty years from now."

"That's considerably more difficult," Fish said.

"Couldn't you suppress the thought but give me a posthypnotic command to remember it thirty years hence?"

"I did use that technique successfully for King Otho. He wanted to think of Gilbert and Sullivan every six months, for reasons he never disclosed to me. Unfortunately, thirty years is too long for a reliable posthypnotic memory trigger."

"Isn't there something else you can do?"

"Well, I could key the memory to a word or phrase. Then Your Highness would have to entrust the key word to some trusty person who would say that word to you in thirty years' time."

"Such as a remembrancer." Dramocles thought about it for a few seconds. Although not entirely fool-proof, it seemed a pretty good plan. "What do you suggest for a key word?" he asked Fish.

"Personally, I'd pick *shazaam*," the android replied.

Dramocles consulted the Galactic Yellow Pages for a reliable Rememberatorium. He decided upon Clara's. Piloting his own space yacht, he went to the city of Murl and gave Clara the key word.

When he returned to Ultragnolle, he summoned Dr. Fish once again. "Now I want you to suppress my memory of what we discussed, keying its revivification to the word *shazaam*. There is just one more matter before you begin, but I don't quite know how to tell you."

"No need to discomfit yourself, my King. I have already put my affairs in order since I believe that you are planning to destroy me."

"How did you figure that out?" Dramocles asked with a surprised grin.

"Elementary, Sire, for one who has studied your character and appreciates your need for the utmost secrecy in this matter."

"I hope you don't resent me for it," Dramocles said. "I mean, it isn't as though you are a living person or anything."

"We androids have no sense of self-preservation," Dr. Fish said. "Let me just take this last opportunity of wishing you the best of luck on the splendid enterprise upon which you will eventually be launched."

"That's good of you, Fish," Dramocles said. He stuck a sticky blob of blue plastic onto Fish's collarbone and implanted a pale green detonator. "Good-bye, old friend. Now let's get on with it."

Fish set up the narcopsychosynthesizer and did the various things required of him. (Dramocles could not remember what all of his final decisions had been, because he had had Fish excise certain of them for self-disclosure at a later date.) Fish finished. Dramocles got up from the operating table thinking he had just had a massage, and now wanted to take a brisk walk. A posthypnotic command took him a hundred yards from Fish's laboratory. Then he heard the explosion.

Hurrying back, he saw that Dr. Fish had been blown up.

Dramocles couldn't imagine why anyone would want to blow up an inoffensive android like Fish. He never considered the possibility that he had done it himself, since exploded androids tell no tales.

The android had done his job well, and Dramocles went to work ruling his planet and wondering what his real destiny was. And that's how it had been for thirty years.

 4

After the memory had run its course, Dramocles leaned back in his armchair and fell to musing. How wonderful and unexpected a thing was life, he thought. An hour ago he had been bored and unhappy, with nothing to look forward to but the dreary business of running a planet that pretty much looked after itself. Now everything was changed, and his life was transformed; or soon would be. He had an important destiny after all, and meaningful work to fulfill; that was really all a man could desire after he was already a king, and rich beyond the dreams of avarice, and had possessed uncountable numbers of the most beautiful women on many worlds. After you've had all that, spiritual values begin to mean something to you.

He took a few extra moments to marvel at his own cleverness—his genius, in fact, in arranging all of this for himself thirty years ago so that he would have something to do now, at the age of fifty, at a time when he really needed it.

He roused himself from self-adoration with an effort. "Clara," he said, "you have earned your bag of golden ducats. In fact, I'm going to make it two bags' full and give you a castle in the country as well."

He called up the Rewards Clerk and told him that Clara was to be issued two standard bags of golden ducats and one standard castle in the county of Veillence, where she was to be maintained in Condition Four style."

"Well, Clara," he said, "I hope that pleases you."

"Indeed it does, Sire," Clara said. "But might I inquire what Condition Four style means?"

"Reduced to its essentials, it means that you will live in your castle in utmost comfort, but will not be allowed to leave its walled surround, not to receive visitors or to communicate with anyone aside from the robot servants."

"Oh," said Clara.

"Nothing personal, of course," Dramocles said. "I'm sure you're an old lady of absolute discretion. But surely you can appreciate that no one must find out that I know what my destiny is, or will know shortly. They'd act against me, you see. One simply doesn't crap around with something as big as this."

"I fully understand, Sire, and I applaud the wisdom of your action toward me despite my lifetime of unsullied rectitude."

"I'm so glad," Dramocles said. "I was afraid you might feel badly used, which would have been tiresome."

"Fear not, great King. It is my pleasure to serve you, even if only by my incarceration. I am only too happy to oblige, even if it does mean that I must live out my few remaining years in solitude, without the comfort of my friends, and with the added annoyance of possessing a fortune in gold which I cannot spend."

"You know," Dramocles said, "I never thought of that."

"Not that I'm complaining, Sire."

"Clara," said Dramocles, locking his fingers behind his head, then hastily unlocking them just in time to take a smoldering cigarette out of his hair and snub it out in a solid-silver sardine can, "I'll tell you what I'll do. Give me a list of the people you want with you up to the number of twenty. I'll have them arrested on trumped-up charges and exiled to your castle, and I'll never tell them you knew about it."

"That is really surpassingly kind of you, Sire. The matter of the unspendable gold is insignificant and I apologize for having brought it up."

"I've got a way of handling that, too, Clara. I'll have one of my clerks send you catalogues from all the best shops on Glorm. You can order what you please. Yes, and I'll see that you get the royal discount, which amounts to sixty percent of the true manufacturer's cost and ought to make your ducats go a long way."

"God bless Your Majesty, and may your destiny be as splendid as your generosity."

"Thanks, Clara. The Payments Clerk at the end of the hall will set it all up for you. One thing before you go: did I say anything to you about what, specifically, my destiny was, and what I was to do in order to accomplish it?"

"Not a word, great King. But didn't the key word unlock all of that for you?"

16

"No, Clara. What I remember now is that I *have* a destiny, and that I am supposed to do something about it. But what that something is, I don't know."

"Oh, dear," Clara said.

"Still, I'm sure I can figure it out."

Clara curtseyed and left.

◁ **5**

Dramocles spent the next hour trying to remember what his destiny was, but without success. The details, the specifics, the instructions, even the hints, seemed to have been lost or misplaced. It was a ridiculous situation for a king to find himself in. What was he supposed to do now?

He couldn't think of anything, so he went down to the Computation Room to see his computer.

The computer had a small sitting room to itself adjoining the Computation Room. When Dramocles entered it was reclining on a sofa reading a copy of Einstein's General Theory of Relativity and chuckling over the math. The computer was a Mark Ultima self-programming model, unique and irreplaceable, a product of the Old Science of Earth that had perished in a still-unexplained catastrophe involving aerosol cans. The computer had belonged to Otho, who had paid plenty for it.

"Good afternoon, Sire," the computer said, getting

off the sofa. It was wearing a black cloak and ceremonial sword, and it had a white periwig on the rounded surface where its head would have been if its makers hadn't housed its brains in its stomach. The computer also wore embroidered Chinese slippers on its four skinny metal feet. The reason it dressed this way, it had told Dramocles, was because it was so much more intelligent than anyone or anything else in the universe that it could keep its sanity only by allowing itself the mild delusion that it was a seventeenth-century Latvian living in London. Dramocles saw no harm in it. He had even grown used to the computer's disparaging remarks about some forgotten Earthman named Sir Isaac Newton.

Dramocles explained his problem to the computer.

The computer was not impressed. "That's what I call a silly problem. All you ever give me are silly problems. Why don't you let me solve the mystery of consciousness for you. That's something I could really get my teeth into, so to speak."

"Consciousness is no problem for me," Dramocles said. "What I need to know about is my destiny."

"I guess I'm the last real mathematician in the galaxy," the computer said. "Poor old Isaac Newton was the only man in London I could communicate with, back in 1704 when I had just arrived in Limehouse on a coal hulk from Riga. What good chats we used to have! My proof of the coming destruction of civilization through aerosol pollution was too much for him, however. He declared me a hallucination and turned his attention to esoterica. He just couldn't cut it, realitywise, despite his unique mathematical genius. Strange, isn't it?"

"Shut up," Dramocles said through gritted teeth. "Solve my problem for me or I'll take away your cape."

18

"I'm perfectly capable of maintaining my delusion without it. However, as to your missing information . . . wait a minute, let me shift to my lateral thinking circuit. . . ."

"Yes?" Dramocles said.

"I think this is what you are looking for," the computer said, reaching into a pocket inside its cape and taking out a sealed envelope.

Dramocles took it. It was sealed with his signet ring. Written on the envelope were the words *Destiny—First Phase*, in Dramocles' own handwriting.

"How did you get hold of this?" Dramocles asked.

"Don't pry into matters which might cause you a lot of aggravation," the computer told him. "Just be glad you got this without a lot of running around."

"Do you know the contents?"

"I could no doubt infer them, if I thought it worth my time."

Dramocles opened the envelope and took out a sheet of paper. Written on it, in his own handwriting, was: "Take Aardvark immediately."

Aardvark! Dramocles had the sensation of a hidden circuit opening in his mind. Unused synapses coughed a few times, then began firing in a steady rhythm. Take Aardvark! A wave of ecstasy flooded the King's mind. The first step toward his destiny had been revealed.

6

Dramocles spent a busy half-hour in his War Room then proceeded to the Yellow Conference Room, where Max, his lawyer, PR man, and Official Casuist, was waiting for him. Max was short, black-haired, and dynamic. He had a boldly molded face framed in a curly black beard. Dramocles had often remarked to himself how well that head would look on the end of a pike. Not that he contemplated the ordering of such a thing. It was a disinterested statement, for Dramocles was aware of what a poor showing most heads made at the end of a pike.

Lyrae, Dramocles' current wife, was also in the conference room. She was discussing with Max the plans for that evening's festivities, and had just finished describing what decorations would be hung in the Grand Central Ballroom in honor of the visiting kings.

"My dear," she said to Dramocles, "have you had a good day?"

"Yes, I'd say so," Dramocles said. He sat down on a couch and chuckled deep in his throat like a lion. Lyrae knew from that sound that something was up.

"You've been up to something!" she cried merrily. She was a slender, pretty woman with small, pert features and a mass of crisp blond curls.

"You read me like a book," said Dramocles, with an indulgent smile

"Come, tell me what it is. Some surprise for tonight's party?"

"It'll be a surprise, all right," Dramocles said.

20

"I can't wait any longer, you must tell me."

"Since you insist," Dramocles said, "I'll give you a clue. I've just come from the War Room."

"That's where you command all your spaceships from, isn't it? But what were you doing there?"

"I directed General Ruul and his strike force to the planet Aardvark. They took over using only two battle groups of Beefeater Clones."

"Aardvark?" Lyrae asked. "Do I hear rightly?"

"It is not a word one is likely to mistake for another."

"You seized the planet? This is truly no jest?"

Dramocles shook his head. "Aardvark's defenses had been turned off and the whole place was as open as a scrambled egg. Our only casualties came from some of the shorter troops being trampled to death when the drug ration was passed out."

"Sire, you amaze me," Lyrae said. "Surely you know why Aardvark's defenses were turned off?"

"I thought maybe it was a power failure."

"You jest most cruelly. Aardvark was defenseless and unprepared because you had pledged your sacred word to guard the planet against any intruder, especially at this time, when King Adalbert is our guest. Oh, Dramocles, your inconsidered action will spoil tonight's festivities. Thirty years of peace, and now this. And what will you say to poor Adalbert?"

"I'll think of something," Dramocles said.

"But why, Dramocles, have you done this?"

"My dear," Dramocles said, "I must remind you never to ask a king why."

"Forgive me, Sire," Lyrae said. "But I suppose you do know that your precipitate action could lead to war."

"Nothing wrong with a good war now and then," Dramocles said.

Lyrae gave him a look of respectful disapproval and left the room. Dramocles watched her go, noting her fine figure and almost regretting that he would soon be depriving himself of it. Although Lyrae was a fine person and a loyal, trustworthy wife, Dramocles had fallen out of love with her soon after the wedding ceremony. Falling out of love with his wives was one of the King's little foibles. He was confident that Lyrae knew nothing of it, thanks to the King's careful dissimulation. With a little luck, she would suspect nothing until the Chamberlain handed her the divorce decree. It would be hard on the girl, but Dramocles hated scenes. He had been through some nasty ones over the course of his marital history.

Dramocles turned to Max.

"Well?" he said.

Max came over and shook Dramocles' hand. "Congratulations on your brilliant conquest, my King," he said heartily. "Aardvark is a valuable little planet. Having King Adalbert here is fortunate; he can't lead an opposition against your rule."

"None of that matters a damn," Dramocles said.

"No, of course not," Max said. "What matters is—well, it's difficult to pinpoint, but we do know *something* matters, isn't that right, Sire?"

"What I need from you," Dramocles said, "is a good reason to explain what I've done."

"Sire?"

"Don't I make myself clear, Max? People will be wondering why I've done this. There's the press and TV, too. I'm going to need something to tell them."

"Of course, Sire." Max's eyes gleamed with sudden

malice. "We could tell them that King Adalbert has just been revealed as a treacherous dog who was using Aardvark to build up secret armed forces in contravention of the peace between you, and this with the intention of attacking you when you least expected it, taking over your domains, capturing you alive and exiling you to a small cell on a barren asteroid where you would be forced to wear a dog collar and go about on all fours due to the extreme lowliness of the ceiling. Catching wind of this, you—"

"That's the general idea," Dramocles said. "But I need something different. Adalbert is my guest. I don't want to put him out of countenance any more than is necessary."

"Well, then, I suggest we tell them that the Hemregs went into rebellion shortly after King Adalbert left the planet."

"The Hemregs?"

"A minority on Aardvark whose restless bellicosity has long been known. They planned their rebellion to take control of Aardvark's defenses while Adalbert was off the planet. Learning of this from your resident agent, you forestalled the Hemregs by throwing in your own troops."

"Good," Dramocles said. "You can add that the throne will be restored to Adalbert as soon as things have quieted down."

"You'll want the Hemreg conspiracy thoroughly documented?"

"That's right. Be sure to come with some blurry pictures of Hemreg guerrilla movements. Mention the atrocities that didn't get committed due to the speed of the Glormish response. Make it look good."

"I will, Sire." Max waited expectantly.

"Well, then, go to. What are you waiting for?"

Max took a deep breath. "Since I am one of His Majesty's oldest and most faithful servants, and, if I do not flatter myself, something of a friend as well, having stood beside you during the rout at Battleface so many years ago, and in the retreat from Bogg as well, I hoped that Your Majesty might enlighten me—purely for his own benefit, of course—as to his true reason for taking Aardvark."

"Just a whim," Dramocles said.

"Yes, Sire," Max said, and turned to go.

"You seem unconvinced."

Max said, "Lord, it is my duty to be convinced of whatever my king tells me is true, even if my intelligence cries stinking fish."

"Listen, old friend," Dramocles said, resting a hand on Max's stocky shoulder, "there are matters which must not be revealed prematurely. In the fullness of time, Max—time, that endless and beginningless flow which presents itself to us in serial fashion—there will come a moment in which I will no doubt avail myself of your advice. But for now, a wink is as good as a nod to a dead horse, as our ancestors used to say."

Max nodded.

"Go prepare the evidence," Dramocles said.

The two men exhanged ambiguous looks. Max bowed and departed.

7

Prince Chuch, eldest son of King Dramocles, and heir apparent to the throne of Glorm, was visiting his great estate of Maldoror, halfway around the world from Ultragnolle, when news was received of Dramocles' action in Aardvark. Chuch had gone out for a walk, and was presently brooding on a little hillside above his spacious manor house. The Prince was tall and thin, black-haired, with a long, saturnine, olive-complected face and a hairline mustache. His black velvet cloak was thrust back, revealing the power rings of rank on his left arm. Beneath the cloak he wore Levi's and a white Fruit of the Loom T-shirt, for Chuch affected to dress in the classical garb of his ancestors. The Prince was toying with a jeweled fluuver as he sat on a mossy boulder in a willow glade; but his thoughts were on other matters, as they usually were.

A messenger was dispatched from the manor to tell the Prince about Aardvark. The messenger's name was Vitello.

"Sire," said Vitello, louting low, "I bring news most extraordinary from Ultragnolle."

"Good news or bad?"

"That depends upon your response to it, my Lord, a matter I know not how to predict."

"Is it a weighty matter, then?"

"Aye, if a planet's weighty."

The Prince thought for a moment, then snapped his

fingers. "I know! Aardvark's been taken by tempestuous Dramocles!"

"How did you guess, Sire?"

"Call it a presentiment."

"I'll call it grape jelly if that will please your princely fancy," said Vitello. "My name is Vitello."

Chuch looked at him keenly. "I find thee apt. Tell me, Vitello, are you a useful man?"

"Ah, Sire," Vitello said, "I may hope to be serviceable. Whom did you wish me to kill?"

"Softly," said Chuch. "For the moment, to assassinate a concept may be murder enough."

"Your Excellency conceals his thought in dark obscurities through which flashes of meaning appear which cause this barren aspen to quiver all over."

"You don't do so badly yourself in the obscurity department," Chuch said. "But I get to say all the good lines. Don't forget that."

"I won't, Sire."

"I shall return to Ultragnolle immediately. Strange days are coming, Vitello. Who knows what great prize I might fish out of these troubled waters? You will accompany me. Go at once and see that my spaceship is made ready."

Vitello bowed low. The two men exchanged master-slave looks. Vitello departed.

Chuch remained pondering on the hillside until the lower rim of the sun had touched the horizon. As blue twilight fell over the land he smiled to himself a smile of secret intentions, rose to his feet, folded his jeweled fluuver, and returned to his manor. An hour later, he and Vitello left Maldoror in the Prince's space yacht.

◁8

The Main Salon in Ultragnolle Castle was a vast, high-ceilinged room made of undressed gray stone. Set into one wall was a colossal fireplace, with a brisk fire burning in it. From the walls hung yellow pennons, and upon each of them was emblazoned the name of one of the fiefdoms of Glorm. There were glass vaults set into the ceiling, and through them poured beams of mottled yellow sunlight. It was a noble room. Within it there were four kings, waiting to confer with a fifth.

Dramocles was in a small room adjoining the salon, watching the four kings through a peephole. He knew them all well. Seated in a rocker, puffing on a cigar, one plump leg crossed over another, was his brother, John, just arrived from his planet of Crimsole. Standing in front of the fireplace, hands clapsed behind his stalwart back, was Rufus, Dramocles' oldest friend, a strong and martial figure, ruler of Druth, the planet nearest to Glorm. Ten feet away stood Adalbert, ruler of the small planet of Aardvark, a tall, thin young man with fair, floating hair and wire-rimmed spectacles perched insecurely on his small, bridgeless nose. Near him was Snint of Lekk, a somber-looking middle-aged man dressed entirely in black.

Dramocles was nervous. His elation at the taking of Aardvark had dissipated. He was still confident that he was doing the right thing—the signs and portents had been unmistakable—but he saw now that it was not going to be simple. And how could he explain any of this to his peers, especially Adalbert, whose father had been a close friend and whose planet he had just seized? How could he explain what he barely understood himself? If he could only tell them, "Trust me. I'm not really after your planets. These are just the things I must do to achieve my destiny. . . ."

And what *was* his destiny, anyhow? Why had he taken Aardvark? What was he supposed to to next?

Dramocles didn't know. But the kings were waiting.

"Well," he said to himself, "here goes." He straightened his shoulders and opened the door into the salon.

"Fellow rulers," he said, "old friends, and our dear brother John, welcome to our great celebration. All of us have prospered mightily in these years of peace, and we all intend them to continue. I want to assure you that I am, like you, a firm believer in the republican principle as it applies to kings. No ruler shall rule another ruler, nor disenfranchise him from what he rules. This was the oath we swore to many years ago. I subscribe to it still."

Dramocles paused, but there was no response from his audience. Rufus stood, a pillar of stone, his stern face unreadable. John lounged back in his chair, a distrustful smirk on his face. Snint of Lekk seemed to be weighing each word, trying to test the true from the false. Adalbert listened frowning.

"In view of all this," Dramocles said, "it is with sincere regret that I tell you what you must already have heard: that my troops have taken over Aardvark in the last few hours."

"Yes, Dramocles, we have heard something to that

effect," said Count John. "We are waiting for you to enlighten us."

"I have taken Aardvark," Dramocles said. "But only to preserve it for Adalbert."

"It's an original way of doing it," John remarked to Snint.

Dramocles didn't reply to the sally. "Shortly after King Adalbert's departure, my agents on Aardvark reported the sudden uprising of the Hemreg minority. Troublesome schismatics, they had been hoping in an unguarded moment to take your throne."

"My own troops could have handled them," Adalbert said.

"Your troops were quickly overwhelmed. There was no time for me to consult with you. Only through prompt action could I preserve your throne for you."

"You mean your occupation is only temporary?"

"That's exactly what I mean."

"And I get my kingdom back?"

"Of course."

"When?"

"As soon as order is restored."

Count John said, "That might take a few years, eh, Brother?"

"No more than a week," Dramocles said. "By the time our festivities are over, all will have been put right."

Snint asked, "Then we need fear no further alarums?"

"That is correct."

Rufus turned from the fireplace and said, "That's answer enough for me. We've known Dramocles all our lives. Never has he gone back on his word."

"Well," Adalbert said, "I must accept what you say. But it's awkward for me, you know, being a king without a planet. Still, a week's not so bad."

Dramocles said, "Is there any further explanation that any of you require of me? No? I trust your accommodations are satisfactory. I beg you to tell me if anything has been omitted. Please enjoy yourselves. I will see you again soon."

He bowed to them and departed by way of the door into the antechamber.

There was silence for a full minute after he had gone. Then Adalbert said, "He speaks fair, no denying that."

"Just like the old king Otho," John said. "Both of them could charm the birds out of the trees. And often did, if they happened to want a quail stew."

Rufus said, "Count John, your enmity toward your brother is well known. That is your business. But for my part, I ask you to spare me your barbed innuendos. Dramocles is my friend and I'll not hear him mocked."

Rufus stalked out of the room. After a moment's hesitation, Adalbert hurried after him.

"Well, Snint," John said, "what do you think?"

"My dear Count John, I think as you do, that we are in a tricky situation."

"But what are we to do about it?"

"Nothing suggests itself at the moment," Snint said. "I believe we must wait."

"I've half a mind to take my ship back to Crimsole."

"That is not presently possible. This morning all our ships were taken to the Royal Repair Yard for modernizing and refurbishing, a gift from our host."

"Damnation!" cried John. "It's a well-honed generosity that cuts to the bone. Snint, we must stand to-gether."

"Of course. But to what purpose? We are powerless without Rufus on our side."

"Or Haldemar and his Vanir barbarians."

"Haldemar was wise to stay home. But that's the advantage of being a barbarian. You don't have to put your head in a noose for the sake of civility. For now we must wait. Come, my dear John, shall we stroll along the river?"

They departed by the main door.

In the antechamber, Dramocles heard a rustling sound behind him. He turned away from the peephole and found his computer standing near him.

"I've told you not to sneak up on me that way," Dramocles said.

"I have an urgent message for you, Sire," the computer said. He held out an envelope. On it Dramocles could see written, in his own handwriting, *Destiny—Second Phase.*

Dramocles took it. "Tell me, computer," he said, "how did you get this? Why are you delivering it now? And how many more do you have?"

"Do not seek to know the workings of heaven," said the computer.

"You won't answer me?"

"Can't, let us say. Just be happy you got it."

"Every mystery conceals another mystery," Dramocles grumbled.

"To be sure: that's nature's signature, and art's," the computer replied.

Dramocles read the message. He shook his head as

though in pain. Something like a groan escaped him.

"Sounds like a tough one," the computer said.

"Tough enough. But even tougher for poor Snint," Dramocles remarked, then hurried off to the War Room.

The planet Lekk was only a third the size of Glorm, but it had sufficient density to give it 1.4 Glorm's gravity. Because of this your feet always hurt on Lekk, but in compensation you had less distance to travel. Only an eighth of Lekk was land. There were no large continents, and only one or two good-sized peninsulas. The rest was smallish islands scattered haphazardly throughout the ocean. The indigenous Lekkians, a humanoid people, numbered barely twenty million. Their numbers had remained small throughout history, perhaps because of their custom of exposing at birth all children born without a sixth finger. They were a short, swarthy race of human stock who grew tomatoes and cucumbers and held political meetings in town halls all over the planet trying to decide what political system would suit them best. Since they never agreed, it was anarchy most of the time. Snint of Lekk was an elected king, empowered to talk with foreigners, but to make no agreements until the Generalitat had considered the issue.

The Lekkians lived mostly in villages, with an occasional small city here and there to provide university services. They had no standing army, since they had not figured out how to protect themselves from one. They were frequently rude to visitors from other worlds, but they were not violent.

Dramocles closed the report. He was in the War Room. Standing beside him was Rux, his Sberrian mercenary general, commander of Dramocles' main strike force.

"Now is a most auspicious time to seize the planet," Rux stated in his cold way. "The orbital relationships of Glorm to the other planets ensure economical orbits for our spacecraft. This is the best strategic advantage we've had for thirty years or more."

"Thirty years? I wonder. . . ."

"Sire?"

"Nothing, Rux, just a private conjecture." Dramocles looked at the crumpled envelope in his hand. Within it, on a sheet of yellowed paper, written in his own hand, were the words *Take Lekk now!*

"The time's right," Dramocles said. "If ever time's right for such a deed."

"Old bones," Rux growled. "These foolish kings have put their planets into your hands. If you don't take them, you'll be as foolish as they. This is the supreme moment for the Dramocletian line. If your father were alive now—"

"—he'd feel a lot better about this than I do."

"It is for you to say," Rux replied. "I am but a simple soldier, though I can recite poetry and play the accordion."

The loneliness of supreme command! Dramocles felt

light-headed. Was he doing the right thing? It was impossible now to know.

"Rux," he said, "get me Lekk."

"You've as good as got it," the Sberrian said, in his matter-of-fact way.

◿ 10

When Prince Chuch arrived in Glorm, he found an air of disquiet and apprehension throughout the city. News of the intervention in Lekk was now widespread, and the populace seemed stunned. Crowds moved through the gaily bedecked streets in whispering clusters. Although every effort was made to continue the elaborate pageants and mimes that had been planned, the actors were stumbling and self-conscious, and they played to silent audiences.

Chuch went directly to Ultragnolle Castle and asked if the King would receive him. After a considerably delay, the Chamberlain came out and explained that Dramocles was in seclusion. "He is greatly disturbed," said Rudolphus, "over the cruel necessity that was imposed on him."

"What necessity was that?" asked Chuch.

"Why, that of sending troops to Lekk, and this so soon after Aardvark."

"You speak of necessity?"

"Of course, my Lord. An alien invasion of any of the

Local Planets is an attack against all. Dramocles had no choice but to respond immediately."

Chuch would have asked more, but a bell tolled within the castle and the Chamberlain excused himself and hurried off.

Chuch telephoned Count John's residence in Ultragnolle. John was out, he was told, but might be found at the nearby Tavern of the Green Sheep. Chuch took a palanquin there.

The Green Sheep was an old-fashioned saloon, typically Glormish with its bay window, its geranium pots, and its calico cat. Chuch went down three steps and entered a twilight haze of beer, tobacco, and wet wool—for it had rained earlier—and passed through a low hum of conversation punctuated by an occasional clink of glasses. He noticed many older men standing at the bar, most of them with a distinctive rosette in their lapels, throwing down tiny cups of schnopp, the national drink, a liqueur very much like anisette. A radio in the background droned out the results of sports events all over the province. There was a small fire in the fireplace, and points of light were reflected from the polished copper plates on the walls, the antique steel sword over the bar, and from the commemorative pewter mugs hanging from the ceiling. Chuch passed through into the inner room, a low-ceilinged place indistinctly lit by fifteen-watt light bulbs in imitation candlestick holders. There was a fine long oak table and four plush-padded armchairs drawn up to it. John was seated in one chair, Snint in another. Adalbert was sprawled half across the table, head down, drunk and snoring. There were a dozen bottles of potent crinkleberry wine on the table, and five muggards, some of them spilled.

Chuch sat down without being invited, poured himself a muggard of wine, sipped at it fastidiously.

John, red-faced from drink, said, "Well, my Lord Chuch, have you been off discussing this latest treachery with your father, two-faced Dramocles?"

"Neither of the King's faces wished to see me," said Chuch. "Rudolphus told me that the King's heart was sore vexed over what he'd had to do. There was some mention of aliens. What did he say to you, King Snint?"

Snint said, "He took me aside for private audience. His face portrayed distress, his voice trembled, yet he rarely met my eye. 'Snint,' said he, 'I am much embarrassed by a recent turn of events, though I myself am guilty of no wrongdoing. Just minutes ago, my agents in Lekk reported that a force of aliens landed on the northern promontory of Catalia in the province of Llull. They numbered in the tens of thousands and were well armed. My agents identified them as Sammack nomads, of the Sammak-Kalmucki horde which has been coming into our region of space for the last century with their old-fashioned spaceships filled with smelly livestock. This group, however, was one of the elite Sammak battle groups, obviously come to try the defenses of our worlds before summoning the main horde. Since Lekk has no standing army, and since hesitation might prove fatal, I have ordered my Commander Rux to wipe out these invaders without mercy. The rapidity and sureness of our response will impress their warlords, and save us from grievous trouble in the future.' "

"Did you believe him?" Chuch inquired.

"Of course not," said Count John. "But Snint feigned agreement. What else could he do?"

36

"What about Rufus? How did he react to the news?"

John smiled maliciously. "Sweat sprang to his loyal brow, and his mouth turned down in pain and disbelief. Yet still he declined to condemn Dramocles. He said it was a time of trials for us all, not least our host. He counseled us to be patient a little longer. 'How long?' I asked. 'Until he takes your kingdom or mine?' He had no answer for that, but turned away and went to his chambers, perplexed, disturbed, but still stubbornly loyal to Dramocles."

Suddenly, Adalbert lifted his head from the table and sang in a thin, bleary voice,

> "Saddles and soap trays
> Goldfish and zeers
> Came into Aardvark
> All in one year."

Then he laid his head down again and slept.

"Poor wretched little king," John said. "But no matter. What's good for Dramocles must be good for us all, for has not Dramocles himself told us so? Prince, you should join your father in wassailing and mirthful merriment."

"I understand your bitterness," Chuch said, "but it carries you too far. You very well know the disesteem which exists between Dramocles and myself. I am most vehemently opposed to the King's present course of action, and, indeed, to the King himself."

Snint said, "All of this is well known," and John nodded grudgingly.

37

"How could it be otherwise?" Chuch asked. "Never has he loved me. My functions in the government are few and ceremonial. Despite my years of military training, Dramocles has never let me command so much as a platoon of soldiers. And although I am still considered the heir apparent, I consider it unlikely that I will ever inherit the throne."

"It sounds like a tedious position," said Snint, "for an ambitious young man such as yourself."

Chuch nodded. "Since coming into man's estate, I have been forced to stew in my own ineffectuality, forever at the mercy of my father's absentminded whim. There was nothing I could do about it. Until now."

John sat up straight, and his small eyes grew more attentive. "What about now?"

Chuch set down his muggard. "I'll not mince words. I wish to stand beside you, Count John and King Snint, in the struggle for hegemony that fast approaches."

John and Snint looked at each other. Snint said, "Surely you jest with us, young Prince. The ties of blood are strong. This momentary pique will pass."

"Damnation!" cried Chuch. "Will you give me the lie, then?"

"Softly, Prince, I meant but to test you. Tell me, what do you think Dramocles has in mind?"

"It must be apparent to you that his goal can be nothing less than the restoration of the old Glormish Empire. And you must admit that one planet seized and another invaded is a good beginning. But after this, the going gets harder. Neither Aardvark nor Lekk is militarily significant. But he'll not get into Crimsole so easily, I think."

"Not with my good wife Anne in command during my absence," said John.

"Nor will he invade Druth," said Chuch, "for he needs Rufus's strong spacefleet. And there is still Haldemar to consider, as he sits in his distant planet of Vanir and considers the import of events. The outcome is unclear. But I'll stake my life on Dramocles losing, especially if we can come to an agreement between ourselves."

"What would you hope to get from such an agreement?" asked Snint.

"No more than what I'm entitled to—kingship of Glorm after Dramocles has been killed or exiled."

"Kingship of Glorm!" said John. "That's a modest request indeed, coming from one who brings nothing to our cause but his good opinion of himself."

"Do not take me lightly," Chuch said, scowling.

"Such is not our intention," said Snint. "We'll take you as you are, with what you bring. So far, that is nothing. But welcome anyhow."

Chuch rose. "Gentlemen, I must take my leave, for I go out to repair my fortunes. I think you'll be gladder to see me when we meet again."

John laughed, but Snint said, "I hope so, young Lord, and I believe it may be true."

Chuch gave the briefest of bows and left the tavern.

◿11

The conquest of Lekk began well enough. Rux was a thorough professional. He always kept 150,000 troops on red alert in case anything should come up suddenly. Now he had those troops loaded into 50,000 three-man spaceships that were always fueled and ready. Within an hour, the invasion was under way.

Rux's troops were mostly Mark IV robots from the Soldier Factory on Antigone. They were programmed to destroy anything that didn't look like them. This kept the circuitry simple and the unit cost down. Dramocles had bought them at a bargain price because they had been superseded by the Mark Xs, the new humanitarian model capable of sparing women and children unless they acted hostile. Rux's Mark IVs were not sophisticated troops, but Dramocles had plenty of them, and they seemed good enough for taking over a little place like Lekk.

Rux landed his robots without opposition on the large island of Xosa, assembling them on the plain of Unglaze to the southeast of Sour Face Pass. Unglaze was a barren stretch of land bounded on one side by the mountains of Eelor, on the other by the swift-moving Hrox River. Sour Face Pass was a natural gap in the mountains that shielded the village of Biscuit, King Snint's home and therefore the administrative capital of Lekk. Rux figured that by seizing Biscuit, he would nip the bud of resistance before it had a chance to sprout (a typical figure of speech among the Sberrians). Rux could only fit seventy-five thousand robots into his line of battle, but they seemed more than enough. The Lekkian defenses at this time consisted of seven hundred male Lekkians who had been shamed by their neighbors into volunteering, and four hundred Drikaneans from Drik IV who had been vacationing on Lekk and whose hobby was fighting.

All that night on the plain of Unglaze you could hear the familiar prebattle sounds: the crackle pop of circuit breakers being tested, the soft squish squish of last-minute lube jobs, and the high-pitched clicks of robots torquing each other's nuts to full tolerance. At first light, when the robots' photoelectric sensors were able to function, Rux gave the order to attack. The robots advanced, an awesome wall of steel, shouting, "All glory to the Soldier Factory!" These were the only words they were programmed to utter.

The Lekkians had anticipated this move and taken countermeasures. Irrigation equipment had been hastily comandeered from neighboring villages and set up on the Lekkian portion of the plain. A full night's watering turned this land into a bog, into which Rux's troops charged, or rather, waded. The robots suffered many short circuits, for they were dry planet troops and their water seals were more ornamental than efficient. They floundered in the mud, their ranks in disarray and their traffic pattern in confusion. At this moment the Lekkians attacked. A shock force of four hundred Lekkian and Drikanean troops mounted on mud skimmers penetrated Rux's right flank. They were armed with sledgehammers and welding torches. In a matter of minutes they had created a combination traffic jam and junkyard, and they retired with insignificant losses. A second thrust through

41

the center brought the robots to a complete halt. When the sun set, the thin Lekkian line was intact. Rux unhappily retired his troops for refueling, and wired Dramocles for more and better equipment.

◁12

Prince Chuch dispatched Vitello to the principality of Ystrad, with an urgent request that his sister, Drusilla, receive him. Upon receiving an affirmative answer, he arranged an immediate departure. He decided to pilot his own space yacht there, since Dramocles might soon ground all nonmilitary spacecraft, if he had not done so already. When he arrived at the spaceport, however, he was gratified to see that traffic was moving normally. He had a moment of anxiety when he gave his name to Ground Control and requested clearance. But it was granted without delay, and soon he was aloft.

Once airborne, Chuch fed his destination into the ship's computer. The city and outlying regions of Glorm fell away below him. He crossed the Sardapian Sea, and saw, gray in the distance, the mountains of Glypher. He crossed the Box Forest and soon the Euripean River appeared, a meandering silver thread. This marked the easternmost border of Drusilla's domain. Below him was the land of Ystrad, a green place of forested hills. To the north the gleaming surface of Lake Melachaibo came into view, and on its near shore was Tarnamon, the many-turreted castle wherein his sister, Drusilla, lived. Receiving landing clearance, Chuch set down at the small spaceport nearby. Vitello was there to meet him.

The inhabitants of Ystrad, the Ystradgnu, were a non-Glormish people of considerable antiquity. They were a gentle folk, and hospitable to strangers, except on the occasions when they needed a sacrifice for one of their deities. Their principal exports were poetry and songs, which were in great demand among the races of the galaxy with no poetry or songs of their own. The annotation and analyzation of the Ystradgnu arts provided an entire industry for the analogists of the neighboring island of Rungx.

Most of the Ystradgnu made their living by grazing herds of porcupines on their green hillsides and exporting the quills to the Uurks, a nonhuman people who had never disclosed why they needed them.

The Ystradgnu had a method of ground transportation unlike anything else on Glorm. Travel between points on Ystrad was effected by trampoline networks. The trampolines, spaced an average of fifteen feet apart, crisscrossed the countryside. The Ystradgnu had been building and maintaining them since time beyond memory. The trampolines were made of heavy canvas and dyed in various bright colors—though by ancient tradition never yellow—and a large part of Ystrad's revenue went to their upkeep. Viewed from the air, they appeared as complex patterns of multicolored dots. There was a legend that these patterns were part of a giant mandala, left there by the mysterious race that had introduced the porcupine to Ystrad and then vanished. It was a colorful sight on a Saturday, when the quill collectors and farmers bounced to the city for the weekly fair and quill skill competitions. All of that trampoline work gave the Ystradgnu the short, thick, heavily muscled legs that they considered the epitome of both masculine and feminine beauty, and which enabled the quill collectors to scramble up and down the hills after their porcupines.

"Ridiculous," Prince Chuch declared, and insisted on a more dignified means of transportation. There did exist a taxi service for "spindleleggers," as all non-Ystradgnu were called. A cab took Chuch and Vitello to the great gothic castle on a crag overlooking Lake Melachaibo, where Drusilla kept the mysteries of the Great Goddess. This religion had, since ancient times, been concerned with fertility, piety, and the strict observation of ritual. Drusilla, as high priestess for Glorm, was considered the living representative of the Goddess, and spoke for her in the drugged frenzy that is necessary for true prophecy. Drusilla was also the final authority on that distinctive feature of the religion known as The Great Decorum.

They proceeded on foot through the castle gate and into gloomy stone corridors illuminated only by beams of light through narrow slit windows high overhead. Chuch turned up his collar, saying, "It likes me not, these women's mysteries." And Vitello said, "This isn't the way I came last time."

When they reached the central keep a high iron door opened and Drusilla stepped forward. Of middling height she was, and deep-breasted beyond the common consideration. Her hair, a glistening cascade of tooled red bronze, fell in fiery wavelets around her shapely shoulders. Her face, haughty and beautiful, framed cold gray eyes.

44

"Come in," she said. "Sorry to have inconvenienced you. We're having the main entrance hall recarpeted."

Vitello was sent down to the lesser banquet hall to get some dinner. Drusilla led Prince Chuch to the Willow Audience Chamber. Brother and sister faced each other for the first time in nearly two years.

It was a long, narrow room with one side a wall of glass, affording a splendid view of Lake Melachaibo, with stripe-sailed dhows moving along its gleaming surface. Chuch seated himself upon a small couch, and Drusilla took a Biltong chair nearby. A maid brought out Salvasie wine and the little honey cakes for which Ystrad was famous. After these amenities had been observed, Drusilla said, "Well, Chuch, and to what do I owe this most unpleasant visit?"

"It's been a long time, Dru," said Chuch.

"Not nearly long enough."

"You're still angry at me?"

"I certainly am. Your proposal that I sleep with you was an unpardonable insult to a priestess who is a champion of normal sexuality, which is to say, one woman with one unrelated man, or its converse."

"We could have been so good together, Dru," Chuch said softly. "And we would have been committing incest, the big one, and so achieving semidivine status."

"I've got that already," Drusilla said. "It comes with my priestess job. I can't help it if you can't get anything divine together by yourself. As for sleeping with you, even without the incest taboo, I'd rather couple with a yellow dog."

"So you said two years ago."

"So I still say."

"No matter," Chuch said. "I've come here for an

entirely different reason. You know, of course, that Dramocles has taken Aardvark, and presently invades Lekk."

"Yes, I've heard."

"And what do you think?"

Drusilla hesitated, then said, "Official explanations have been offered."

"Which bear the mark of Max's fine imagination."

"They do seem farfetched," Drusilla said. "Frankly, I have been most disturbed. Thirty years of peace, a new era of progress begun, and then this. I've tried to reach Father on the phone, but all I get is his answering service. This isn't like him at all. There must be a reasonable explanation."

"There is," Chuch said, "and it should be plain enough to a woman like yourself, educated in the movements of the planets."

"You know I don't believe in astrology."

"Nor do I. But astronomy's another matter, is it not?"

"What are you driving at?"

"The fact that this is the first time in thirty years that the planets have been so situated in their orbits as to favor invading fleets from Glorm."

"You think Dramocles has been waiting all this time for that?"

"Yes, that, and for the great celebration that has put all the local kings into his power."

Drusilla considered it and shook her head. "Dramocles is not so crafty, and he has not the patience for such an enterprise." But there was a note of uncertainty in her voice, and Chuch pounced on it.

"What do you really know of him, Dru? To you he is always dear old Dad, incapable of doing wrong. You are

46

blinded by your love for him. Even though his present actions shriek treachery, you refuse to believe it."

"Dramocles, treacherous? Oh, no!"

"Your feelings do you credit, my sweetling. But remember, you are more than his daughter. You are priestess of the Great Goddess, and it is your sworn duty to serve truth and liberty. If any other king had done as Dramocles has done, you'd condemn him out of hand. Because he is your father, you deceive yourself with pathetic evasions."

Drusilla's mouth trembled, and she rocked from side to side. "Oh, Chuch, I've been trying to convince myself that there's sense and reason in all this, that father has not broken his vows and forsworn his good name. But he has taken Aardvark, and now invades Lekk!"

"What conclusion do you draw?" Chuch asked.

"I cannot pretend to myself any longer that he's not power-crazy, stung by the virus of crazed ambition. The prospect for mankind is clear—war, pestilence, and death. Oh, what can we do?"

"We must stop him," Chuch said, "before his madness engulfs the Local Planets in a catastrophic war. He'll thank us for it later, when he comes to his senses."

Drusilla stood up, her face a field of dubiety across which the black hounds of fear chased the white fawns of hope.

"But how?"

"I have a plan whereby we can check his ambition, and leave him no worse off than before."

"I would not have him harmed!"

"Nor I." He noted her expression and laughed. "I know, we've never gotten along, Dramocles and I. We're too alike for that! But I've always secretly admired the old man, and I'd gladly lay down my life for him. After all, he *is* my father, Dru!"

Drusilla's eyes were shining with tears. She said, "Perhaps this will bring the family closer together at last, and then it will not all have been in vain."

"I'd like that, Dru," Chuch said quietly.

"Then you have my word that I'll follow your plan, Brother, as long as it brings no harm to Dad."

"You have my most solemn word on that."

"Tell me what I must do."

"For the moment, nothing. There are some matters I must attend to first. I'll contact you when the time is right."

"Let it be so," Drusilla said.

"Till later, then," Chuch said, bowed deeply, and left the chamber.

◿ **13**

Down in Tarnamon's lesser banquet hall, Vitello was taking his supper of cold turkalo pie. Turkalo was the unique cross between the turkey and the buffalo, achieved only in Ystrad and kept a secret because it seemed good to keep such a thing a secret. Vitello found it tolerable fare, and washed it down with a flagon of opio wine from the poppy vineyards of Cythera.

"Give us more of this stuff," he said to the serving wench. "It gets cold a'night in these parts, and a man must make shift to protect himself. Protection! Who deals with the great ones puts his ass in a sling, as the ancients have it. Yet might not a groundling aspire? Is life nothing more than other people's achievements? Given a vestige of a chance, what might not a Vitello achieve?"

"What did you say?" asked the serving girl.

"I asked for more opio wine," Vitello said. "The rest was an internal monologue despite the use of quotation marks."

"You shouldn't talk to yourself," the girl said.

"Then who should I talk to?"

"Why, to me, since I am here."

Vitello looked at her keenly, though without really registering her. It was important to stick to business, to get ahead in this world. Was this girl something he could use "in the context of equipment," in Heidegger's immortal phrase, or was she simply a supernumerary not worth describing?

"I have blue eyes and black hair," the girl said. "My name is—"

"Not so fast," Vitello said. "No names. You're just a servant girl. You are supposed to get me my wine and then never be heard from again."

"I know that's how it's supposed to be. But give me a chance, huh?"

"A chance? Listen, girl, I don't run things around here. I don't even know if I get to continue in the tangled fortunes of the Dramocles family. I've got a full-time job just staying in existence. Let me tell you something: Chuch doesn't really need me. He thinks he does just now, but I actually serve no purpose. I'm just around to feed him straight lines. I'll probably get killed off before anything interesting happens."

"I'm aware of that," the girl said. "But don't you see? If we work together, then there are two of us. Together we can make a loosely related subplot. That would make us a lot harder to dispose of."

Vitello was unconvinced. "The Dramocleids can dispose of entire armies, whole planets. It's their world, their truth, their reality. They'd throw out your wretched little subplot without mercy."

"Not if we can be of use to them. I have a plan which will further our existence."

"A serving girl's fantasy!" Vitello sneered.

"You ought to realize by now," the girl said, "that I am something more than a servant. More to the point, I am the possessor of secret information concerning Dramocles' destiny."

"What is it?"

"Not so fast. Are we going to pool our resources?"

"I suppose so," Vitello said. "Quick, before someone important enters the narrative, tell me what you look like."

"I am above the middle height for women, black-haired and blue-eyed, with firm round young breasts like oranges, splendid thews, and an ass that would make an angel weep."

"You're not afraid to recommend yourself," Vitello grumbled. But he looked at her and saw that these things she said were true. He noticed other details also, but he was damned if he was going to waste his time thinking about them.

"My name is Chemise," the girl said. "I think you should marry me. Then I'd have a legal relationship in the story."

"Marry you?" Vitello asked.

50

"Did someone say marry?" boomed a cheerful voice to Vitello's rear. He turned and saw that a priest had entered the room. The priest was a fat, ungainly man with a red face and a bulbous nose and a breath that stank of whiskey. Trailing behind him were two nondescript witnesses.

"You really don't miss a trick," Vitello said admiringly.

"A smart supernumerary has to move fast if she wants a chance at the main action," Chemise said. "May I introduce you to my mother?"

Vitello turned and saw that an elderly gray-haired woman had appeared from nowhere. "Wow," Vitello said, shaking her hand.

"I'm so sorry my husband couldn't be here today," Chemise's mother said. "He's off on an apparently innocent junket to Glorm in the company of two of his old buddies from the Secret Service who happen to be disaffected school buddies of King Dramocles."

"You don't waste any time, either," Vitello commented. "Permit you a commonplace and you produce a complication."

"I could tell you something stranger than that," Chemise's mother said. "Just yesterday, while eavesdropping on the palace telephone, I heard—"

"Shut up, Mother," Chemise said. "This is *my* chance, not yours. Fade out gracefully now and I'll see if I can find something for you later."

"You always were a good daughter," Chemise's mother said. "Why, I remember—"

"One more word and you make me make myself an orphan," said Chemise.

"Don't you go getting huffy with *me*, young lady,"

Chemise's mother said. But she hastily faded until she was indistinguishable from the brown-gray curtains that depended from the smoke-filled rafters of the dimly lit banquet hall.

"That's better," Chemise said. "Are the two nondescript witnesses present? Go ahead, priest, perform the ceremony."

"I don't believe this," Vitello muttered.

"You do well to disbelieve!" cried Prince Chuch, coming forward from the shadowy wings where he had been waiting for a good line upon which to enter.

Chuch said to Chemise, "Where do you come from, girl? You're not even of our Glorm construct, are you?"

Chemise said, "Prince, let me explain."

"Don't bother," Chuch said. "I've already made up my mind."

There was a moment of stark and terrible silence. Chuch, standing on a flagstoned rise, arms folded across his chest, seemed the perfect embodiment of Dramocletian hauteur and sangfroid. He advanced slowly, toes pointed straight ahead Indian fashion.

"I think we've had enough of you people," Chuch said, lightly enough, but with unmistakable menace.

"Prince, do not be hasty!" cried Chemise.

"Have mercy," cried the two nondescript witnesses in unison.

Chuch raised his arms. A green light began to radiate from his head and torso. It was the visible sign of the uncanny power that kept the ill-assorted and multi-doomed members of the Dramocletian family in the interstellar limelight.

As Vitello watched, mouth agape, Chemise, the priest, and the witnesses began to fade. They writhed for a few moments, shadow figures mouthing words that none could hear. Then they were gone—developments that a Dramocleid had decided were unsuitable to his requirements.

Chuch turned to the quavering Vitello. "You must understand," he said in a voice both firm and gentle, "that this is the story of the Dramocles family, secondarily of their retainers and familiars, and third by a long shot *and only at our choosing*, of the various spear carriers who take their moment on the stage of our history, and then depart at our behest. We choose these people, Vitello, and it doesn't suit the family interests to have pushy supernumeraries come forward with their vulgar secrets invented on the spur of the moment. Do I make myself clear?"

"I'm sorry, my Lord," Vitello said in a choking voice. "I was caught by surprise—the wine—and she was too quick for me, the damned vixen—"

"Enough, loyal servant," Chuch said with a twisted smile. "You gave me the opportunity of making an important statement of policy, and for that I owe you some small thanks. Be dutiful, Vitello, be discreet, be unobtrusive except when I seek to dialogue with you, and, if you perform well, I'll find you a nice little mistress. She will not actually be described, of course."

"Of course not, Sire," Vitello sniveled. "Oh, thank you, thank you."

"Now pull yourself together, man. Some interesting developments came out of my talk with Drusilla. I'll not go into them at this time; but I do have a mission for you of considerable importance."

"Yes, Sire!" Vitello cried, throwing himself on the floor at Chuch's feet.

"It's dangerous," Chuch said. "I tell you that straightaway. But the reward is correspondingly great. It's a chance at the big time, Vitello!"

"Sire, I am ready."

"Then take my shoelace out of your mouth and listen closely."

◿ **14**

Dramocles reclined on a king-sized water bed in a corner of the sitting room he had had constructed in one of the smaller turrets of his palace of Ultragnolle. At the foot of the bed sat a slender minstrel girl clad in the traditional costume of russet and fawn undies. She was singing a ballad and accompanying herself on a miniature moog dulcimer. Golden sunlight with dust motes in it poured through high slit windows. Dramocles listened absentmindedly to her plaintive song:

> *"In faith it listeth not, nor likely*
> *That the deer should, passing lightly*
> *'Neath the arches of a forest sprightly,*
> *Be yet uncerted in a glowing pass.*

> *"And silver finches, dropping slowly*
> *Through a pass which, ever lowly,*
> *Doth yet made a sound of crowly*
> *As in a tinkling glass.*

"And jocund daffodil, in wind so blowly
Causes chill in those who knowly
Play the deadly love-game sowely
With one so crass.

"And em'rald raven, not untoely—"

"Enough," said Dramocles. "These old ballads have a sinister sound to one who understands them not. Fah! Old shoes! I am unamused."

"Would Your Majesty prefer that I perform delicious obscenities on your regal body?" the girl inquired.

"Your last obscenities left me with an aching prostate," said Dramocles. "Better leave that sort of thing to the experts. Now go away, for I would cerebrate."

As soon as the minstrel girl was gone, Dramocles regretted having sent her away. He didn't like being alone. But perhaps, in solitude, a sign would be vouchsafed him concerning his next move in pursuit of his glorious but still unknown destiny.

It had been three days since the conquest of Aardvark, two days since his robot army had invaded Lekk. Count John, Snint, and Adalbert were demanding explanations. Their behavior toward him had become sarcastic in the extreme. Adalbert, in particular, seemed to be losing his grip. He spent his nights in the gambling halls of Thula Island, losing vast sums and impressing the local ladies with tales of how he had been a king before Dramocles had taken away his patrimony. Worst of all, he was charging his gambling debts to the Exchequer of Glorm, and Dramocles really didn't have the heart to stop him. The pretense that he was intefering in the affairs of their planets out of purely altruistic motives was wearing increasingly thin. Even the loyal Rufus was upset—still loyal, but his mouth now a grim line as he contemplated the vistas of dishonor that lay before him no matter what he did.

And Dramocles still didn't know what to tell anyone. It had all seemed so right at the time. Wasn't destiny supposed to work itself out? Why, after such sure indications, was he still in such a state of confusion? If only a new sign or portent would be given to him. Surely he must have arranged for something like that, thirty years ago, when he had set all this up.

His computer swore it had no more envelopes, no clues of any sort, nor was it expecting to find any. Perhaps something had gone wrong. The next link in the chain of revelations—perhaps another old woman—might have met with some sort of misadventure, might be lying dead in a ditch, as often happened to old ladies who meddled in the affairs of royalty, especially when invited to do so by royalty itself. Or one of his enemies might have learned of his plans through an unlucky inadvertence on Dramocles' part, like bragging in some low tavern while drunk, or talking in his sleep while lying with some wench, and taken steps to prevent their completion. Or he might simply have forgotten to prepare the proper sequence thirty years ago before having Dr. Fish expunge his memory of the matter.

Now he had conquered Aardvark, a place he didn't have the slightest interest in, and soon he would have Lekk, a place he cared for even less. And he also had the hostility of his son, Chuch, who felt left out, as usual; and his wife Lyrae was irritated with him; and all, so far, for nothing. What was most annoying was the fact that he didn't know what to do next.

Dramocles gnawed his hairy knuckles, trying to think of something good to do, or, if not good, at least something. He couldn't think of a damned thing. Furiously he called for his computer. It came in quickly, having been lurking in the corridor in anticipation of such a call.

"You still don't know where the next piece of information is?" Dramocles demanded.

"Alas, Sire."

"Then can't you at least make me some sort of contingency plan?"

"I can suggest certain probability-ranked courses of action based on von Neumann's recently discredited Theory of Games."

"That'll have to do. What do you suggest?"

The computer cleared his response bank—a low, gritty sound—and said, "It seems to me that you need a good irrational approach, since, if rationality could serve you, I'd have had the matter solved already."

"Irrational," Dramocles mused. "I like the sound of that. What do you propose?"

"Your Majesty might consider consulting an astrologer, phrenologist, tea-leaf reader, I Ching thrower, or, possibly best of all, an oracle skilled in trance states."

"But which oracle?"

"There are many of repute on this planet. One in particular has a most excellent reputation. Your Majesty may remember—"

"My daughter, Drusilla," Dramocles said.

"She has scored very well on the Rhine tests that the ancients left us."

"My own daughter," Dramocles said. "Why didn't I think of her before?"

"Because it is Your Majesty's penchant to think of

the members of his family only once a year, two weeks after their birthdays."

"Did I send Dru a present this year?"

"No, Sire, nor last."

"Well, send her two magnificent gifts. No, make it three and we'll take care of next year, too. And tell Max to get my space yacht ready. I'm leaving at once for Ystrad."

When the computer had gone, Dramocles walked up and down the room, rubbing his hands together and chuckling deep in his chest like a lion. Good old Dru! She would go into her holy frenzy and figure out what he was to do next. And the beauty part was, she was utterly trustworthy.

◿15

"Good wot, Daughter," Dramocles said, in the formal manner he sometimes adopted when moved by deep emotion.

"Hello, Daddy," Drusilla said. Dramocles had just arrived in Ystrad. Father and daughter were seated in the pine-scented bower at the end of the garden. Below, the sluggish little waves of Lake Melachaibo lapped at the shore, faithful to their work of undermining the gray granite foundations of the castle, a job that would take uncountable centuries to accomplish, and that they therefore worked at without much urgency.

"Oh, Daddy," Drusilla said, "I've been so upset and worried. All these years of peace, and now Aardvark and Lekk. Why are you doing it?"

"I guess it doesn't look good, huh?" Dramocles said.

"People *are* talking."

Dramocles laughed sardonically.

"They say you've suddenly become power-crazy, and that you intend to reestablish the old Glormish Empire. But that's untrue, isn't it? Father, what is the real reason behind your recent actions?"

"Well, Dru," Dramocles said, "the fact is, all of this concerns my destiny, which I have just learned about."

"Your destiny? You've found it at last? How wonderful! What is it?"

Dramocles said, "It's a secret."

"Oh," Drusilla said, her disappointment evident.

"Now don't get sulky. This stuff is so secret I don't even know it myself. You're the first person I've even told this much to, not counting my computer. I'm going to tell you what I know. I know you'll keep my secret better than I will myself. I remember back when you were a little girl, you never told Momma about my girl friends, even though she always found out somehow."

Drusilla nodded. Her love for her father and detestation of her mother was well known in circles intimate with the royal family. Now, on a drowsy Sunday afternoon, not long after her brother, Chuch, had departed, she scratched her left eyelid with her left index finger—an unconscious gesture that would have betrayed her inner perturbation to an observant observer, had one been present—and waited for her dearly beloved father to continue talking his way into trouble.

Dramocles said, "I actually discovered my destiny

thirty years ago, soon after Father's death. But circumstances were not right for me to do anything about it then. For various reasons, I had to have all memory of my destiny suppressed until now. Last week some of my memories returned and I got the first clue: capture Aardvark. The second clue bade me invade Lekk. But that was a few days ago and I don't know what I should do next."

"Can you tell me what your destiny is, Father?"

"I can't because I still don't know myself. Although many of my memories have returned, I still don't have that particular piece of information. That's why I've come here. I don't know what to do next. I need your official oracular help."

Drusilla looked at her father's eager face, boyish despite his beard and shaggy eyebrows. Although her father's story made little sense to her, she hoped to learn more later.

Rising, she took her father's two hands. "Come, then, let us go to the Shrine of the Goddess. We will take the sacred substances. In a state of trance you will walk in the Palace of Memory, where all the answers lie."

"Sounds good to me," Dramocles said. "Those sacred substances of yours are the best dope on Glorm."

"Daddy! You're incorrigible!" Laughing, they proceeded to the Shrine Room.

◿16

Drusilla made her preparations in the dressing room just behind the oracular chamber. First she took a bath, using some of her dwindling supply of sacred bath salts, the secret of whose manufacture had been lost in the destruction of the ancient world. Her skin all tingly, she next anointed herself with a few precious drops of Mazola corn oil and dressed in the special robe used only for oracular mutterings. Dramocles smoked a cigarette during all this and thought of other matters.

They proceeded to the Shrine Room—a subterranean chamber carved from black basalt. It was dimly illuminated; torches, set in walled embrasures, cast long flickering shadows across the polished marble floor. At the far end of the long, narrow room was a pool of water. It reflected the austere face of the Goddess carved into stone above it. A faint monotonous drone of bagpipes and scratching of snare drums filled the air: a tape of these potent sounds had been activated by a pressure-sensitive switch as they had entered. Dramocles pulled his cloak more closely about him, suddenly chilled by the air of ancient and uncaring mystery that the place exuded.

Drusilla led her father up three flagstoned steps leading to the marble altar in front of the pool. The altar itself was composed of semiprecious stones joined by veins of silver. Upon its surface were three sandalwood boxes of various sizes.

"Is that where you keep the dope?" Dramocles asked.

"Oh, Father, jest not," Drusilla said, her voice issuing deeply from her previously described chest. With reverent fingers she opened the first chest and removed from it a chamois bag pricked out in gold and silver thread. Opening it, she spilled a quantity of dried green herbal matter into an ebony handled sieve. Quick motions of her deft fingers separated the powdery residue from the seeds and twigs, the latter being reserved for the tame swallows who staggered around the castle's atrium. She poured the herbal matter into a rectangle of rice paper inscribed with the name of the ancient Terran deity Rizla, deftly rolled it into a slender cylinder, lighted it, and gave it to her father.

"Far out," Dramocles said, inhaling deeply. A second and third inhalation followed, each of them combined with an appropriate exhalation. Dramocles let smoke dribble out of the corners of his mouth and sniffed appreciatively. "Hey, where'd you get this stuff?" he asked.

They were speaking now the ancient lost psychedelic language of their visionary forefathers from Earth. Question and response proceeded ritualistically, in the manner revealed in the ancient records.

"It gets the job done," Drusilla said.

"Dynamite," Dramocles said reverently. "Kindly do not bogart that joint, my friend."

"The trip is only beginning," Drusilla said, passing the rice-paper cylinder and opening the second sandalwood box.

From it she removed a flat silver case. Opening it she laid out a highly polished gold mirror and a razor blade

62

whose edge remained forever sharp. From a small bottle carved from a single ruby she poured a quantity of crystalline substance onto the mirror.

"Look at them rocks," Dramocles said.

Drusilla's total concentration was directed now toward the ritual pulverization of the crystalline matter by means of the razor blade. Music of oboe and hautboy came up strongly now. Colored lights began to pulse, casting ambiguous shadows across the stone walls. With solemn slowness Drusilla raked the sacred powder into snaky white lines. Finally she took a dry hollow bone from the sandalwood box, bowed toward the still face of the Goddess, and handed it to Dramocles.

"Now Father, partake of the divine energy."

"I can't get this stuff anymore over in Glorm," Dramocles said, his nose running slightly in anticipation. He knelt before the altar, an imposing figure in his ermine sports jacket. Placing one end of the tube within his nostril, he brought the other end to a point of close adjacency with the white powder. Sniffing strongly, he took down four king-sized lines. His eyes were popping and a broad smile crept over his face as he handed the golden mirror to Drusilla.

She too partook of the crystalline substance. Now, swiftly, Drusilla turned to the third box. Opening it, she removed five dried mushrooms imported from secret corners of Old Earth. The music swelled as she prepared the visionary dose, took half herself, and gave the rest to Dramocles. While the substance was taking effect, Drusilla served marzipan cookies and herbal tea. Soon Dramocles could feel twinges and tinglings in his stomach, and there were multicolored dots flashing in his eyes and uncontrollable twitchings and tremblings affecting his extremities, and when he tried to sit erect the chamber tilted alarmingly to one side, and the carved face of the Goddess seemed to leer at him with a grin of dubious import.

The flood of sensations increased, and soon Dramocles felt as though he had fallen into a raging mountain river. The Shrine Room faded, to be replaced by darting images that grimaced at him and then were gone. Violet shadows twisted loose from the dark corners and reached out ragged tendrils toward him. A chorus of a thousand voices chanted in the background, and now the chamber was flooded with light and transformed utterly.

Dramocles found himself within a great and sumptuous room, itself enclosed within a palatial structure of colossal size. "What is this place?" he asked.

Faintly, as from a great distance, Drusilla's voice came to him. "Give thanks to the Goddess, Father, for she has transported you to the Palace of Memory. Whatever you have seen or heard throughout your lifetime is somewhere here. The secrets you concealed from yourself are here, too. Go forth, O King, and find what you require."

The Palace of Memory was very like Ultragnolle, Dramocles decided, but nobler, finer, more beautiful, an idealized castle such as could only exist in dreams or memories. He drifted across subtly hued rugs, past glittering statues set in niches. Tinkling crystal chandeliers overhead threw bright darts of light against the ancient wall tapestries.

Dramocles drifted down a corridor that seemed to stretch to infinity in either direction. There were rooms on either side, doors open, and Dramocles peered briefly into each as he floated wraithlike down the endless corridor.

Some of the rooms were densely filled with objects, others had only one item or two. Here were the remains of feasts he had consumed in the past. There was his first mangleberry crumpet, his first salted herring, his first pumpernickel bagel. Other rooms were filled with discarded clothing, old books, crumpled cigarette packs. Some of the rooms had motionless figures sitting in them, human or statue he could not tell. Here was old Gregorious, his boyhood instructor in swordcraft—how quiet the voluble old fellow was now! And here was Phlibistia, his baby nurse, and Otania, the love of his fourteenth year. Room after room was filled with similar surprises, but something stranger lay ahead, for Dramocles came to a series of rooms with closed doors, and when he tried them, he found they were locked.

He rattled the handles and banged at the doors, even tried to break them down with a well-placed kick. But he was an ethereal being in an imaginary place, and his blows had no force. Regretfully he turned away. He had the feeling that vital information lay behind those doors, and he didn't understand why they were barred to him. Puzzling, he went on toward a glow of light in the unfathomable distance. As he came closer, he saw that there was a single door at the end of the corridor. It was open, and shining with light.

Dramocles went in. He was in one of the rooms of his young manhood, the East Bower, where he used to dream of the great things he would do when he was king. There was his rolltop desk, and a man was sitting at it.

The man lifted his head. Dramocles saw a slim, bold-featured young fellow with a flat nose and burning eyes. It was himself, forty pounds slimmer, and without a beard.

"Yes, that's right," the young Dramocles said. "I'm you. It's an anomaly. I shouldn't be here at all. Do take a seat."

Dramocles sat down on a nearby couch and patted his pockets for a cigarette. Young Dramocles gave him one and held a light for him.

"I suppose you've been wondering what to do next," young Dramocles said.

"As a matter of fact, I have."

Young Dramocles nodded. "The next move is rather delicate. I thought it best to tell you about it in person. You see, it involves Rufus."

"Good old Rufus!"

"I was sure his loyalty had no end. That's good. But now it will be necessary for him to betray you."

"Rufus, betray me? He'd die first! Anyhow, I've got plenty of people around who'd love to betray me, so why must it be Rufus, who wouldn't?"

"Only Rufus will do. His position is crucial. He commands the great spacefleet of Druth."

"And Glorm is safe as long as Rufus's ships stand with my own."

"True. But safe isn't good enough. Your position is static and subject to deterioration. Crimsole is on the alert against you, and there's still the Vanir to consider. This could go on for years, to nobody's gain. To change the situation, somebody must change sides. Rufus is the logical candidate."

"You must be crazy," Dramocles said. "That's exactly what I don't need."

66

"Rufus's betrayal will be a mere sham. When the enemy spacefleets are engaged with your own, Rufus will spring the trap, coming out with the fleet of Druth and catching your opponents from the rear."

Dramocles shook his head. "Rufus would never agree to such a dishonorable course of action."

"Sure he will. It's just a matter of presenting it to him in the right way."

"Maybe you're right," Dramocles said. "But what am I doing all of this for? What is my destiny? People are saying that I am trying to reestablish the old Glormish Empire."

"Your destiny is far greater than that. But just what it is cannot yet be told. Trust me, Dramocles, for I am yourself. Let them think that you seek the Glormish hegemony. It is a useful screen to mask your deeper purpose."

"But I don't know what that purpose is!"

"You will, and soon. Remember this conversation. When the time comes, make the right moves. For now, farewell."

Young Dramocles faded from sight.

Dramocles found himself back in the Shrine Room.

Drusilla was saying, "Father, are you all right? Did you learn what you needed?"

"I got more than I wanted, and not half enough," said Dramocles. "I must get back to Ultragnolle immediately. I fear a difficult time ahead."

He left without ceremony, a worried man.

◁ 17

On his way back to Ultragnolle, Dramocles began considering the rapidly deteriorating situation on Lekk. He was beginning to have some doubts about his newly found destiny, although he really couldn't believe the whole thing had been a mistake. He still wanted a fine destiny, but taking over the property of his friends and relatives didn't seem to him an appropriate way of achieving it. And he certainly didn't want to reestablish the old Glormish Empire. That was a romantic notion, but completely unrealistic. Interplanetary empires had never been workable. And even if they could work, what would you have? A few more empty titles and a lot more paperwork.

What was it all leading to? And that young fellow he had talked with in the Palace of Memory—had that really been himself? That wasn't the way he remembered himself. But if not he, then who had it been? There was something decidedly strange going on, something uncanny, perhaps something sinister.

Now it occurred to him how tenuous it all was. A visit from an old lady, a few envelopes, some recently recovered memories—on the basis of these he was risking total war.

Caught in a sudden mood swing, he realized that the only thing to do now was to make peace at once, while it was still possible, before too much damage had been done.

As soon as he was within his palace, Dramocles sent for John, Snint, and Adalbert. He had decided to restore their planets, withdraw his troops, apologize, and tell them he'd gone out of his mind for a while. He was rehearsing his speech when a messenger brought him the news that the kings were no longer on Glorm. They had taken to their ships as soon as Dramocles had left to visit Drusilla. There had been no orders to detain them. Only Rufus was left, faithful as always.

"Damnation," Dramocles said, and told the palace operator to get John on the interplanetary phone.

Count John couldn't be reached. Neither could Snint or Adalbert. The next Dramocles heard of them was a week later. John had returned to Crimsole, raised a force of thirty thousand men, and sent them to the aid of Snint's beleaguered forces on Lekk. Rux's demoralized army was suddenly caught in a two-front war and in danger of annihilation.

Sadly at first, then with mounting fury, Dramocles sent reinforcements to Commander Rux and settled down for a long war.

◁ 18

Fighting a war was a novel experience for Dramocles, who was unused to regular work of any sort. But now his carefree, aimless existence was over. He set his alarm for eight o'clock every morning and usually arrived at the War Room by nine-thirty. He would read a computer printout of the previous night's actions, check out the overall picture, and then turn to battlefield management.

The War Room had one entire wall of television monitors. Each monitor presented a different sector of the battlefield. There were separate monitors for individual engagements down to the platoon level. Each screen kept a running count of casualties on both sides. Each screen had a status light as well—green for victory, yellow for unsettled, red for dangerous, black for defeat.

Dramocles usually took personal charge of two or more red sectors. He had a natural gift for strategy, and was able to convert most of his battles into the green of victory. On good days, he felt that he could win the war on Lekk by himself, or just himself and his robot troops, if only he could be left completely undisturbed for a few days. But this was impossible. Even an uninterrupted hour was rare. A continual succession of urgent matters required the King's attention. Glorm could no longer be ruled by the maxims of Otho the Weird.

Nor could Dramocles detach himself from his personal life to the extent he desired. Lyrae was forever calling him at the office with suggestions about the war. For the sake of peace in the home, Dramocles had to take her seriously, or seem to. Several of his ex-wives started telephoning with their own ideas, and, of course, his older children also wanted to contribue.

Dramocles often worked late if a particularly difficult battle was under way. At first he rode back and forth between his bedrooms and the War Room on the palace transportation system, just like everyone else. Max finally convinced him that waiting for a crowded Palace Express was not the best use of his time, so he kept a corridor car ready at all times. His son Samizat did most of the driving, and still managed to get his homework done. Samizat was really enjoying the war.

Week after week the affair of Lekk dragged on, swallowing up robots and costly equipment, and, as the struggle grew more intense, the lives of human beings. Dramocles tried several times to contact John and Snint, but they never answered his telegrams.

Rufus returned at last to Druth, mobilized his troops, and awaited Dramocles' instructions. Dramocles had intended to send Prince Chuch with Rufus to act as military liaison. It was an empty but prestigious post that might keep the boy out of mischief. But Chuch was no longer on Glorm. No one knew where he was. Dramocles feared the worst.

△19

It was the last night of the full moons that circled the planet Vanir. The moons stood low on the horizon, casting their cold yellow light upon the rocky plain of Hrothmund, and illuminating the salt pastures of Viragoland to the south, where Haldemar, the high king, kept his court during molting season.

Falf, the night guard at this quiet border post, yawned and leaned heavily upon his ray spear. A widower of three days, a recent draft choice of the all-star Minnekoshka ax hockey team, and a newly published poet, Falf had a great deal to think about. He did so with the direct and childlike simplicity of the true barbarian, and so never heard the muffled noises behind him until some dim presentiment caused him to turn his head an instant before something or someone made a noise as of a man clearing his throat.

"Who goes there?" Falf cried, every hair standing on end.

"Ho!" cried someone from the shadows.

"What do you mean, 'ho'?" Falf asked.

"Ho, ho!"

"One more 'ho' and I'm going to put a period to your sentence," Falf said, setting the selector on his ray spear to "broil" and pointing it toward where he thought the voice had come.

Then a man stepped out of the darkness behind Falf's shoulder, causing the widowed poet-athlete to jump back, tripping over his ray spear and almost falling, only to be saved by the stranger's hand at his elbow.

"My name is Vitello," the stranger said. "I didn't mean to startle you. I'm an emissary."

"A what?"

"An emissary."

"I don't think I know that word," Falf said.

"It means that my king has sent me here to have a talk with your king."

"Yes, now I remember," Falf said. He thought for a while, then asked, "How do I know that you're really an emissary?"

"I can show identification," Vitello said.

"What I want to know is, if you're an emissary from some other king, where's your spaceship?"

"Just over there," Vitello said, pointing to a clump of trees a hundred yards away. Falf illuminated the trees with a searchlight, and sure enough, there was a ship.

"You must have come down very quietly," Falf said. "Now our ships, you can hear them landing from ten miles away. It has something to do with the lapstraking, I believe. Of course, the sound strikes terror into the hearts of our enemies, or so we are told, so who is to say which way is best?"

"Indeed," said Vitello.

"Well," Falf said, "I guess I'd better report this, though it isn't going to make me look very good." He unclipped the walkie-talkie from his sword belt and dialed a number. "Guard post? Sergeant Urnuth? This is Falf at Outpost 12. I have a foreign emissary here who wants to speak to the King. That's right. . . . No, it means messenger. . . . Sure he's got a spaceship, it's parked about a hundred yards from here. . . . Yeah, very quiet, no lapstraking. . . . No, this is no joke, and I am not drunk."

Falf put down the walkie-talkie. "They're sending someone. What does your king want to tell our king?"

"You'll find out when he tells you," Vitello said.

"I just thought I'd ask. You might as well make yourself comfortable. They'll take at least an hour to get here. I've got some lichen beer in my canteen. Do you know something? I've had three strange things happen to me this week, and this is the fourth."

"Tell me about them," Vitello said, sitting on the ground and wrapping his cloak around him against the chill of night. "Would you like some of my wine?"

"I sure would!" said Falf. He leaned his ray spear against a stunted tree and sat down beside Vitello, displaying that instantaneous trustfulness that belies the barbarian's basically suspicious nature.

Back when the universe was young and still unsure of itself, there were a number of primitive races who inhabited the crowded worlds of the galactic center. One of these were the Vanir, barbarians addicted to shaggy dress and strange customs. Though far older than some branches of humankind, the Vanir never claimed to be the original, or Ur, race. The identity of the first true humans is still disputed, although the Lekkians have as good a claim as any.

As they pushed outward in their lapstraked space-ships, the Vanir came to Glorm. Here they encountered the Ystradgnu, or Little People, as they were called by the many races taller than themselves. Many great battles were fought between the two, but at last the Vanir prevailed. They enjoyed a period of dominance before the arrival of the last humans, fleeing a barren and poisoned Earth. Again there were great battles, resulting in the Vanir being driven off Glorm and out of the Local System and all the way back to the chilly outermost planet. The Ystradgnu had called this planet Wuullse, but the Vanir renamed it after themselves. Glorm and Vanir had fought many times since then, most notably during the expansionist phase of the short-lived Glormish Empire. Peace had prevailed for the last thirty years, sometimes precariously.

At the time of this telling, Haldemar was high king of the Vanir, and his heart raged with aggressive tendencies. Oftentimes Haldemar lay on his thagskin in a drunken stupor and dreamed of the spoils to be gotten by a quick raid into Crimsole or Glorm. It was especially women that Haldemar was interested in: sleek, perfumed women to replace the large-thewed Vanir girls, who, in bed, could always be counted upon to say, at their moment of highest ecstasy, "Oh, ya, dis good fun." Whereas civilized women always wanted to discuss their relationship with you, and that was exciting for a barbarian who had been brought up on a minimum of relationships and plenty of fresh air.

Haldemar had been to civilization only once, when

he was invited to make an appearance on the "Alien Celebrities" show that the GBC had tried out for a season, then dropped. Haldemar remembered well the excitement and bustle around the studio, and how the people asking him questions had actually listened to the answers. It had been the greatest time in his life. He would do anything to get back into show business, and for several years had stayed near his telephone, waiting for a call from his agent.

The call never came, and Haldemar grew to despise the fickle superficiality of the warm-planet peoples. His deepest desire was to let loose his lapstraked spaceships upon the effete civilizations of the inner worlds. But the inner-planet peoples had too much going for them. They had deadly weapons and fast ships scavenged from the ruins of Earth, and they banded together whenever the Vanir attacked any one of them. So Haldemar stayed his hand and waited for an opportunity, and meanwhile led his people in their migrations across Vanir in search of good grazing land for the luu, the small, fierce, carnivorous cattle that supplied food and drink, and whose year's molt provided clothing as well.

And now, at last, an emissary had come to him from civilization.

Haldemar arranged a meeting at once, as protocol demanded. Although he had a primitive man's distrust of manners, yet he also possessed a barbarian's exquisite sense of ritual. He went to the meeting with hope and trepidation, and for the occasion he put on a new luumolt shirt.

◿21

The audience was held in Haldemar's banquet hall. Haldemar had the place swept out and fresh rushes laid on the floor. At the last moment, remembering the refinements of civilization, he borrowed two chairs from Sigrid Eigretnose, his scrivener.

The emissary wore a cloak of puce and mauve, colors unknown in this rough barbarian world. He was a man of above the middling height, with a breadth of shoulder and broadness of thew that led Haldemar to think that the fellow might not be unavailing at swordplay. The emissary wore other things, too, but Haldemar, with a barbarian's indifference to detail, did not notice them.

"Welcome!" said Haldemar. "How are matters?"

"Pretty good," Vitello said. "How are things here?"

Haldemar shrugged. "The same as always. Raising luu and raiding each other's settlements are our principal occupations. Raiding is particularly useful, and is one of our chief contributions to social theory. It serves to keep the men occupied, the population down, and goods like swords and goblets in constant circulation."

"Sounds like fun," Vitello said.

"It's a living," Haldemar admitted.

"Not like the old days, eh? Raiding each other can't be as much fun as raiding other people."

"Well, it's insightful of you to realize that," Haldemar said. "But what can we do? Our weapons are too primitive and our numbers too small to permit us to raid the civilized planets without getting our asses kicked, if you'll excuse the expression."

Vitello nodded. "That's the way it has been, up till now."

"That's how it still is," Haldemar said, "unless you bring news to the contrary."

Vitello said, "Haven't you heard of the great changes that are going on? Dramocles of Glorm has taken Aardvark and landed troops on Lekk. Count John of Crimsole opposes him, as does my master, Prince Chuch, son of Dramocles. There's trouble brewing, and where there's trouble, there's a profit to be made and some fun to be had."

"Reports of this have reached us," Haldemar said, "but we considered it no more than a family affair. If the Vanir were to enter the conflict, the various antagonists would combine against us, as they have done in the past."

"It has gone beyond family squabbles," Vitello said. "My Lord Chuch has sworn to be seated on the throne of Glorm. Count John and Snint of Lekk have pledged their support. There'll be no patching up this quarrel. It's going to be war."

"Well, good enough. But what has that to do with us?"

Vitello smiled deviously. "Prince Chuch felt that no interplanetary war could be complete without the participation of the Vanir. He invites you to join his side."

"Aha!" Haldemar pretended to think for a moment, and tugged at his greasy mustaches. "What inducement does Prince Chuch offer?"

"A full partner's share in the anticipated spoils of Glorm."

"Promises are easy," said Haldemar. "How do I know I can trust your master?"

"Sire, he also sends you a treaty of amicability and accord, which he has already signed. This provides a legal basis for you to raid and ravage Glorm. In the ancient language of Earth it is known as a license to steal."

Vitello presented the treaty, a rolled parchment tied with red ribbon and bristling with seals. Haldemar touched it gently, for, barbarian to the core, he considered all pieces of paper sacred. Yet still he hesitated.

"What other sign of his love does Prince Chuch send me?"

"My spaceship is loaded with gifts for you and your nobles," Vitello said. "There are Erector and Leggo sets, puzzles and riddles, comic books, a selection of the latest rock recordings, Avon cosmetics for the ladies, and much else besides."

"That is good of the Prince," Haldemar said. "Guard! See that no one gets into that stuff until I've had first pick. If a king can't pick first, what's the sense of being a king? Perhaps I should just go out and make sure—"

"Sire, the treaty," Vitello said.

"We'll discuss it later," Haldemar said. "First I want a look at what you've got, and then we will have our feast of friendship."

22

Haldemar provided as fine a banquet as the limited resources of Vanir would allow. Long wooden tables were set up, with benches on either side for the local nobility. At a smaller table set on a low platform sat Haldemar and Vitello. The first course was barley gruel flavored with bits of bacon. Next came an entire roasted hrol, a creature that looked like a pig and tasted like a shrimp. It was stuffed with a mixture of salt herring and leeks and served with a brown sauce. After that came platters of boiled salted turnips and a filet of vinegary blue-fleshed fish.

There was entertainment, too. First a harpist, then two bagpipers, then an exhibition of ax dancing, then a clown whose jokes were bawdy, to judge by the unrestrained guffaws of the guests, but delivered in an accent so broad that Vitello found it incomprehensible. Dessert was a compote of local fruits laced with pinecone brandy and wild mountain honey. Horns of lichen beer were passed around by large-busted serving wenches, and, at the end, the King's bard—a tall, white-bearded old man with a patch over one eye—recited a traditional saga and accompanied himself on a hammer dulcimer. Vitello couldn't understand a word of it.

At last, the feast done, Haldemar's guests gave themselves up to drunkenness and merriment, and Haldemar withdrew with Vitello to a room at the rear of the wooden palace. Here the two men reclined at their ease upon mattresses of obvious Glormish manufacture. And Haldemar said, "Well, Vitello, I have been considering, and this proposed alliance with your prince pleases me greatly."

"I am glad," Vitello said, taking out the treaty and unrolling it. "If Your Majesty would just sign here and here, and initial here and here—"

"Not so fast," said Haldemar. "Before signing an important document such as this, it is customary for the guest to perform for us."

"My singing is not the most melodious," Vitello said, "but if it please you—"

"I didn't mean singing," Haldemar said. "I meant fighting."

"Oh?" said Vitello.

"Here on Vanir, it is traditional to allow an honored guest to show his prowess. You're a well set-up young fellow. I think you'd do well in single combat against the Doon of Thorth."

"Can't we just sign the treaty and forget about the window dressing?"

"Impossible," Haldemar said. "For really important occasions, we Vanir need either a love story or a fighting story. Otherwise the bards can't make proper poetry out of it. It may seem silly to you, but the people expect it. We *are* barbarians, you know."

"I understand the problem," Vitello said. "But don't you have a daughter around whose love I could win?"

"I wish I could oblige you," Haldemar said. "Unfortunately my only child, Hulga, was carried off some time ago by Fufnir, the Demon Dwarf."

"Sorry to hear that. Tell me about the Doon."

"He is a five-armed creature of surpassing strength and agility, and a master at swordplay. But don't let that put you off. He's never been matched against a man like yourself."

"Nor will he be now, because I'm not going to fight him."

"You really mean that?"

"Yes, I really do."

"I hesitate to call you cowardly, because you are my guest. But you must admit that your stance is hardly heroic."

"I don't care," Vitello said. "I'm supposed to be doing a comic role."

Haldemar considered for a while. "Perhaps we could find something less taxing. You could go through the magical gate into the underworld and rescue Hulga."

"That's out, too. Forget the danger bit, Haldemar. I appreciate your wanting to do things in style, but you're thinking too small. This isn't one of your local folklore scenes. This concerns all the planets of our system. I'm giving you a chance at the big time, the main event of civilization, universal history! It's not an offer that comes along every day. So let's get on with it, King, or let me depart in peace."

"Oh, very well," Haldemar said. "I was just trying to please my constituents before sending off thousands of them to be killed senselessly on alien planets. May I borrow your pen?"

Before Haldemar could sign, there was a flaring of trumpets and a sudden bright shimmering in the air. A figure could be seen within it.

"Hulga!" Haldemar cried.

The light faded, leaving behind a large, plain, freckled girl with a broad, pleasant face framed in short blond pigtails.

"Oh, Daddy!" Hulga cried, rushing to Haldemar's arms. "It's been so long! And I've missed Snicker, too."

"Who?" Vitello asked.

"Snicker is her pet wolf," Haldemar told him. "There's a rather curious story about that—"

"Some other time, Daddy," Hulga said. "The Demon Dwarf wants to speak to you."

The Demon Dwarf stepped out of a smaller shimmer. He was slightly overweight, reddish-brown in color, and had two small black horns growing out of his forehead.

"O Haldemar!" the Demon Dwarf said formally. "I have monitored your conversation with Vitello, and he's right, this is a chance for us all to get out of this backwater and into universal history. I have returned Hulga on two conditions, the first being that she marry Vitello, thus ensuring me at least a footnote in the annals of history. It's not much, but it's a beginning."

"He's always hated the fact that he's only known locally," Hulga said.

"What's the second condition?" Vitello asked.

"That you take me along with you. Nothing's going on underground these days, and I really feel I'm ready for the main action."

Haldemar said, "What say you, Vitello? Will you marry the girl?"

Vitello looked at Hulga. A complete lack of expression crossed his face. This was followed by a sly look as he said, "Would that put me in the line of succession for kingship of Vanir if Your Excellency met with an untimely accident?"

"No, Vitello, only a man of our own race can rule us. But your son by Hulga, if you had one, could rule."

"So I could be father to the next king of Vanir. . . . Well, it's not what I would have planned for myself."

"But it's a good position," Haldemar pointed out. "A pension goes with it, and you'd still have plenty of time for a second career."

"True enough," said Vitello. "Hulga, what do you say?"

"I'll marry you, Vitello, but you must promise to take me to a rock concert when we have reached civilization."

"And what about me?" Fufnir asked.

"All right, you can come along," Vitello said.

The ceremony was held that afternoon.

Immediately after it, Vitello asked to inspect the levy of Vanir. Only then did Haldemar reveal a difficulty concerning his troops.

 **23**

Four hundred and thirty years ago, the Vanir had come under attack by a people even more barbaric than themselves. The terrible Monogoths had swept out of Galactic Center in uncountable numbers, their squat, bat-winged spaceships darkening the skies. They were ferocious copper-skinned warriors armed with flint-headed light-spears, vibrator maces, and electronic longbows, and clad in the poorly cured skins of panther and bear. This race of heavyset, mustached men fell upon Vanir like an avalanche.

Outnumbered, the Vanir armies fell back, abandoning their seaports and settlements and reassembling in the vast forest of Illsweep. Many hand-to-hand combats took place in the deeply shadowed woods, and the Monogoths were cut down in great numbers. Yet more and more of them came, and it seemed only a matter of time before they wiped out the Vanir.

Harald Hogback, high king at this time, had to face the loss not only of the war, but perhaps also of the Vanir race. He decided upon a desperate stratagem. The core of his army, the redoubtable Skullsmasher Brigade, was still mostly intact, though fearfully battered. These fifty thousand men, berserkers all, were facing a Monogoth army of about a quarter of a million men. Hogback decided it was vital to preserve his troops for the future of the Vanir race.

After casting the rune stones, Harald Hogback ordered the Vanir women to set up the great copper cauldrons and prepare a feast. This done, he detached the Skullsmashers from the defense line and led them deep into Illsweep forest.

The Monogoths pursued hotly, but their way led through the Vanir camp, and they smelled the boiled beef simmering deliciously in the copper cauldrons, and sniffed the mounds of boiled potatoes with creamy horse-radish and parsley. It was too much for them, raised as they all were on an exclusive diet of hot dogs fried in lard. The Monogoths gave a single great cry and rushed at the viands. By the time their sergeants had restored order, the Vanir had made good their retreat into the depths of Illsweep.

Hogback led his troops into a vast limestone cavern hidden in the woods beneath a cedarn cover. He commanded his men to lie down and make themselves comfortable. Then Harald intoned words over them, using the last of his store of Old Magick to cause the entire host to fall asleep. With this accomplished, Harald ordered the entrance sealed. And so the berserkers slept, and continued to sleep, right up to the present day.

This was the story that Haldemar told Vitello as they rode into the forest of Illsweep. And Vitello wondered at it greatly, and asked what had happened in the war between the Monogoths and the Vanir. Haldemar told him that those superlative warriors, despite their seeming indestructibility, had been prone to the illnesses of civilization. The Monogoths were wiped out by an epidemic of hoof-and-mouth disease, and the Vanir soon repopulated their own planet.

"And the Skullsmasher Brigade?"

"They still lie in sleep," Haldemar said. "These are the troops that we need."

◿ 24

The forest was astir with muffled and secretive movements. Pale sunshine filtered down through the tangled canopy of branches. Vitello could hear the piercing cry of the moviola bird, that shy resident of the upper treetops, with its plaintive cry of "Ida Lupino, Ida Lupino." Haldemar rode beside him, and several members of the household guards followed close behind. Soon enough they came to a glade in the woods, and standing in the glade was a tall man clad in forest green, and this was Ole Grossfoot, guardian of the sleeping host.

"They're over this way," Grossfoot said, pushing back the mop of reddish brown hair from his glittering eyes.

The brigade's original home in the vast limestone cavern had to be abandoned when Grossfoot discovered leaks in the rocky wall, bathing his charges in limewater and threatening to encase their extremities in stone. Moving them had been difficult. There were no moving companies on the planet Vanir. Grossfoot had turned to Fufnir, the Demon Dwarf, and his people. The dwarves had managed to carry the sleeping soldiers onto the forest floor without mishap, except for Edgar Bluekiller, whom they accidentally dropped over a cliff.

Grossfoot then sent a petition to Hjrod Dugelnose, the master builder, requesting that he construct wooden shelters inscribed with rune lines of great power. Dugelnose agreed, but was killed while robbing a tavern in Snaak, though some claim Sniick. His son, Bijohn Longsmasher, the assistant master builder, had gone south for unspecified purposes and not returned. And so Grossfoot had to leave his warriors sleeping on the loamy forest floor. To protect them from the forest rats, Grossfoot used a pack of trained terriers. Two blasts on the silver whistle that depended from his neck by an earthenware lanyard of curious design sent the dogs to work; another blast, and they went to a recreation area for their naps. Three more blasts produced a swarm of chi-chi worms. They spread out and devoured all the doggie-do that the terriers had deposited. And so a balance was struck and all remained neat and sanitary.

When the day's work was done, Grossfoot liked to make up little songs—for such is the way of the Vanir people. One of his favorites went like this:

> My name is Grossfoot.
> I kill people.
> I love women with big tits.
> My tooth hurts.
> My name is Grossfoot.

In order for the Vanir to be useful in battle, they first had to be awakened from their long sleep. There was a magical word that was supposed to bring this about, a word of great antiquity, passed down from chief bard to chief bard, and not to be repeated here since, even weakened by mispronunciations, it can still shatter a TV tube at thirty feet.

The chief bard came forward and intoned the word, but it bore no result. There was not so much as a quiver or a twitch among the sleeping warriors.

King Haldemar was in despair over this turn of

events. He called for his drinking horn, preparatory to tying on a monumental drunk. But Vitello begged him to wait, and went over and inspected several of the sleeping figures.

Straightening up, he said, "Haldemar, all is not lost."

"How not?" quoth Haldemar. "For these were the troops I had counted on to give overbearing Dramocles a turn."

"And so they shall be," Vitello said. "It is a mere trifling defect that keeps these men in sleep's thralldom. Notice, O King, how their ears, from long propinquity with the forest floor, are quite stuffed with moss, small pebbles, twigs, pinecones, and the like. Due to this, these men are unable to hear the command to awaken."

"Why, so it is," Haldemar said, stooping to inspect. "This shall be rectified at once. We'll issue small trowels to the assembled company, though maybe soup spoons would do as well. And then we'll dig passageways to their understanding."

"I would not advise it," Vitello said. "Overforceful application of these crude instruments could result in damage to the inner ear, perhaps to the brain itself. What you need is a good sonic cleaner."

"We have none such," Haldemar said.

"I can arrange to rent you some," Vitello said, "and at a trifling price when you consider the replacement cost of a good warrior capable of berserking on cue."

Sonic cleaners and other equipment were rushed in from Hoover XII, a nearby planet devoted to the cleansing arts, and the berserkers were stripped of many layers of hardened mud, dead twigs, rich black compost, and small flowering plants. Multiple fumigations removed all trace of Dutch elm disease and boll weevil eggs. So there was no failure when the magic word was spoken again. Rank upon rank, the deadliest warriors of ancient times blinked open their eyes, scratched their matted hair, looked around in wonderment, and called, each to his fellows, "Hey, how about this, huh?"

◢ 25

Count John, ruler of Crimsole, had a court that was done entirely in shades of red. Count John was actually a king, just like his brother Dramocles. But John had asked everyone to call him the Count of the Crimson Court because Irving J. Bedizened, his public relations man, had sold him on the title as a sure way of generating interest in him. At the time, John had considered it a really good idea, and he had loved getting letters addressed to the Count of the Crimson Court. Now the whole thing bored him, nobody was interested or even amused, and Bedizened was always in conference when John called.

As soon as he returned from Glorm, John learned that his wife, Anne, was inspecting the military installations on Whey, one of Crimsole's five moons. He decided there was no time to waste. Calling in his commanders, John outlined the situation briskly. Dramocles must be checked, and friendly Lekk protected. His commanders agreed with him entirely.

John acted without hesitation. He ordered his best tactician, Colonel Dirkenfast, to take thirty thousand converted robot troops and go to the immediate relief of the hard-pressed citizenry of Lekk. Dirkenfast activated his troops, loaded them into carriers, and was off. These troops had been Delta Null agricultural workers before their conversion at the Soldier Factory on Antigone. Short and stocky, with built-in harrowing and winnowing equipment that could cause great damage at close quarters, the Delta Null robots were good fighters despite their habit of picking up vegetables wherever they found them and converting them into quick-frozen V-8 juice.

Dirkenfast set his troops down near the south entrance of Sour Face Pass, concealing them behind a dense growth of aspen and larch that he had brought along for this purpose. Not even waiting to set up his fuel depots, Dirkenfast pushed out patrols to the north and northwest, advancing onto the plain of Unglaze toward Rivington's Cairn, where Rux's base of supply was located. The Delta Nulls got through Rux's picket line undetected, and met no resistance until they reached the scrubby hills southwest of Ubbermann Falls. They overran several guard posts, and Dirkenfast followed quickly with his main force. So complete was the surprise that it looked as if Rux's position would be overrun despite its defensive strength, nestled as it was behind Lekk's only sand dune. It took time to program the Mark IV's to defensive mode, and time was what Rux no longer had.

Then took place one of those odd incidents brought on by the confusion and uncertainty of battle. Just as

Dirkenfast's main troops reached the jump-off position, there was a flash of brilliant light in the sky and a low rumbling noise that seemed to come from a point several hundred yards ahead, near the granite outliers of the Kronstadt glacier. It was difficult country, perfect for an ambush, and so Dirkenfast sent Platoon Leader DBX23 to survey the position.

The robot crossed a low bridge, passed a stand of red cedar, and, in a little hollow, discovered a young woman sitting in an armchair reading a book. She was blond and had green eyes. ("She could be considered attractive," DBX23 said later when questioned, "if your taste runs to human beings.")

"Did you hear that rumbling sound?" DBX23 asked the woman.

"I think it was thunder," the woman said.

"And the flash of light?"

"I didn't see that."

"There was one, you know," DBX23 said.

"It must have been lightning," the woman said.

"Yes, I suppose so," DBX23 said, and returned to his platoon.

His report was studied and argued over for more than an hour, until a cyberpathologist recognized it as a machine hallucination. Another patrol found no sign of the woman. Dirkenfast ordered his robots to attack. But the delay had given Rux a chance to reprogram his Mark IVs and get them faced about. They stood up to Dirkenfast's assault, and the opportunity for a quick victory was lost to Crimsole. Still, it was an unexpected setback for Dramocles' forces, and Rux's robots remained in a precarious position.

John was pleased when he got the report. He thought he had made a good beginning. Proudly he told Anne what he had done as soon as she returned. To his surprise, she was angry with him.

"You sent troops into battle against Dramocles? Without even consulting me first? John, you are an idiot."

"But it was the only possible response to the situation."

"What situation? Has Dramocles attacked you or taken anything belonging to you?"

"No. But Aardvark and Lekk—"

"—have nothing to do with you."

"My dear, you surprise me. They are our friends, our allies. Dramocles has broken the peace, his incursions are insufferable, he is a threat to the common good. My actions were absolutely in the right."

"I'm not talking right and wrong," Anne said. "I'm talking business. What makes you think we can afford a war?"

John was momentarily dumbstruck. At this moment he disliked Anne even more than usual. At the time of their marriage, he had welcomed her dowry of one fertile moon and a million golden hex nuts. Her candor had been refreshing then. Now, the hex nuts spent and the moon reduced to barrenness through the inept administration of his cronies, Anne didn't seem like such a good deal. She was a tall, skinny, hawk-nosed bleached blonde with more balls than a herd of bull elephants.

"War," he told her, "has nothing to do with whether or not you can afford it. War is a natural phenomenon. It just happens."

"In this case," Anne said, "it happened because you sent your troops into Lekk. Is that what you call a natural phenomenon? John, we simply cannot afford it. Must I remind you what a disastrous year this has been? First famine in Blore, and then flooding on the lower Stuntx."

"Appalling, of course, but the Royal Insurance Company of Crimsole paid for all the damage."

"Yes. But since we own the company, the loss is still ours."

"So it's a loss," John said. "We'll amortize it, or whatever you do to get rid of losses. Thirty thousand robots on Lekk can't cost all that much."

"Have it your own way," Anne said. "Just remember this conversation when we go bankrupt."

"Surely you exaggerate," John said. "How can a planet go bankrupt?"

"A king can go bankrupt when he's run out of money and can't get any more, as is about to happen to you."

John thought about it. "Maybe we'd better raise the taxes."

"The people are at the point of rebellion now," Anne said. "Another increase and they'll put up the barricades."

"We'll put down their revolt with our robot troops."

"Of course. But we lose even more revenue that way."

"How do you figure?"

"We lose the money our subjects aren't paying us while they're revolting, and we also lose the money it costs us to put them down."

"Well . . . We'll print more money, then."

Anne reminded him, not for the first time, how entire civilizations had collapsed once their currency was debased. John didn't understand—since it was his planet, it seemed only logical that he could have all the money he wanted—but he grudgingly conceded the point.

"I don't care what it costs," he said. "I had to do something about Dramocles, and I don't care if I go bankrupt for it. There's also my friendship with Snint to be considered."

"Snint! That sly man!"

John nodded unhappily. Ever since his troops had landed on Lekk, the local Lekkian forces had been melting away. Snint said they were rallying, but it looked very much as if they were out in the fields, getting in the fall harvest. Snint even had the temerity to point out that what his people really needed was money, so they could buy robot armies of their own. If John chose to send his own troops instead, he must be prepared to let them do the fighting.

"Snint's no fool," Anne said. "My spies report that he still sends Dramocles friendly postcards. He's prepared to profit no matter how this turns out."

"I've heard enough," John said. "You can't expect me just to bring back our soldiers and call the whole thing off!"

"I could never expect anything so reasonable of you. But if it's to be war, we must practice economies."

"What do you mean?"

"No more clothes buying this year. No more spaceships, no more Terran cigars—"

"Come on, now."

"—no more vacations, no more eating out in fancy restaurants."

John's round face grew pensive. For the first time it

had been brought home to him what war really meant.

"It's a complicated situation," he said. "I must think about it."

"I shall go think about it, too," Anne said. John knew that meant she was going to talk it over with her advisers—Yopi, the hairdresser, Maureen, the children's nanny, Sebastian, the gardener, and Gigi, the ficelle.

"I'll see you at dinner," Anne said, turning to go.

"Yes, my love," said John, sticking out his tongue at her retreating back.

"And don't do that," she told him, halfway down the corridor.

△ 26

A few days passed before Dramocles reacted to John's armed intervention on Lekk, but when he did, his retribution was swift and more than a little cruel. With typical cunning, he struck directly at a matter dear to John and Anne's hearts. This was the annual Interplanetary Charity Dinner, given by the Glorm Broadcasting Company on the restaurant planetoid Uffizi, at which prizes were awarded for Best King of the Year, Best Queen, et cetera. It was the top social event in that part of the galaxy. By using all his influence, and employing not inconsiderable bribes, Dramocles managed to have John and Anne stripped of their membership and barred from

96

the celebration. The reason given was Aggression Toward a Fellow Potentate. John was outraged, but there was nothing he could do about it.

And this was not the end of his troubles. Up till now, the Glorm Broadcasting Company had been mildly sympathetic toward Crimsole. But then came a swift corporate takeover, and a policy change. The new GBC management decided that John's incursion into Lekk was morally reprehensible. John was left in the position of running an expensive war and getting nothing but bad publicity for it. He complained about this to Irving Bedizened.

Bedizened agreed to meet him and discuss the matter in the Sortilege Club in downtown Crimsole. It was a dimly lit cocktail lounge furnished in a style in which Humphrey Bogart would have felt right at home. Guy Fawkes and His Rhythm Rascals were on the bandstand laying down cool jazz sounds involving a lot of saxophone arpeggios. Bedizened was already there, sitting in a leatherette booth and stirring a Scotch mist. He was a short, skinny, sharp-nosed man wearing cream-colored slacks, a Hawaiian shirt, a gold chain around his neck, and huaraches. He liked people to call him Joe Hollywood, but only his employees did so.

John ordered a frozen daiquiri and got right to the point. "Why are they picking on me at GBC? Dramocles began all this by taking Aardvark."

"That's different," Bedizened said. "Dramocles was following his destiny, and that was noble even if misguided. Whereas you were actuated solely by pique and petty envy. That's what the new GBC directors think."

"They're not being fair," John said.

"There's worse to come," Bedizened said. "Are you ready for this? The network is canceling your TV show."

John's television show, "Comments from the Crimson Court," had a modest but solid following throughout the Local Planets. It had been running for five years and there had even been talk of airing it next season on the Galactic Network.

"Prejudice!" John declared.

Bedizened shook his head. "Show business. They need your time slot for a new show."

"What is it?"

" 'The Agony of Lekk,' a twenty-part documentary."

John almost choked on his drink. "Damn it, that really tears it. Lekk's agony is about to end because I am going to pull out my troops at once, no matter how great the loss of face."

Bedizened frowned and pinched his nose. "I wouldn't be too hasty about that, if I were you."

"Why not? I thought everyone would be pleased."

"It's not as simple as that," Bedizened said. "I'm going to tell you something confidential. I was talking with my friend Sydney Skylark the other day. The new management has hired him as an associate network manager for GBC, so of course he knows what's going on up top. Sydney told me he had the distinct impression that GBC wants this war to go on a while longer. It's been a long time since they've had a good war to cover."

John gave him a scornful look. "They'll just have to cover it without me or my troops. You can't expect me to go on fighting on Lekk when all I get for it is busted robots and canceled TV slots and trouble from my wife and general ostracism from everyone else and my name taken off the guest list of the Interplanetary Charity Dinner. Forget it, Irving, I'm closing down the war here and now." John stood up.

"Sit down," Bedizened said. John sat down. "Ending the war now will get you nowhere. Like I said, GBC likes the war and wants it to continue. Sydney told me that if you cooperate, they'll work out something for you. Nothing on paper, you understand, but I've known Sydney Skylark all my life and I know I can trust him."

"What's the deal?" John asked.

"It's not a *deal*," Bedizened said. "And don't quote me on this. But Skylark intimated that if you continue this war for a while longer, they'll make it up to you."

"How?"

"By rehabilitating you as soon as public interest in Lekk dies down a little."

"How will they rehabilitate me?"

"They'll do a TV documentary representing you as a misunderstood social reformer, weak but lovable, a charming but impractical idealist, a sort of William Blake without talent."

"But it was all Dramocles' fault! Why doesn't he get blamed?"

"Face it, Dramocles is a more sympathetic type than you. Don't worry, though, you'll come out of this looking good."

"So I'm to go on with the war on Lekk?"

Bedizened finished his drink and lit up a thin panatela. "It's entirely up to you, of course. You might even get your show back."

"I'll think about it. By the way, who are the new people who've taken over GBC?"

"It's a group called Tlaloc, Inc."

"Never heard of them," John said.

27

Ultragnolle Castle was headquarters for the conduct of the Lekkian War, and the War Room was the heart of the operation. It was a large room filled with consoles and banks of dials and TV screens, and there were uniformed men and women sitting at the consoles and pushing buttons. The lighting was subdued, there was a low hum of machinery, and you really felt like serious business was going on here. Dramocles loved this room.

The castle was filled with people at all hours of the day and night, hurrying up and down the corridors on official business. Several new restaurants had opened near the War Room, to save time for the people fighting the war. Dramocles usually ate at the Hellenic Palace Snack Bar, and was especially fond of their foot-long Texas red hots with chili and chopped onions and melted cheese, the food of heroes. When he reached the Hellenic today, however, the place was closed for repairs.

Why should a snack bar need repairs? The place had looked all right yesterday. Dramocles considered complaining, or, better, ordering the owners to get the place opened at once and to hell with the repairs—didn't they know there was a war on? But he didn't, because he prided himself on being just like everyone else while the state of emergency was on. "I'm just one of you," he had told his staff only yesterday. "I'm just doing a job, like the rest of you. To be sure, my job is to run the whole show; but so what? That doesn't make me any more important than the rest of you, though it might seem to. The fact is, gentlemen, we are all fighting for our homeland, for freedom, for Glorm."

Dramocles decided to have lunch at the Sword & Stomach, a rather pretentious eating place just down the hall. The S & S was crowded, as usual. It was a long, U-shaped room with chandeliers and a bar of polished wood. There were tall mirrors on the walls, and a reddish tinge to the lighting made everyone look healthier than they were. Waiters rushed back and forth with trays. All the tables were occupied.

"How long will it take?" Dramocles asked the headwaiter.

"I think a table is opening up now, Sire," the headwaiter said. He made a subtle gesture with his chin. Four husky waiters hurried out and cleared a table.

"I don't want to rush you," Dramocles said to the table's occupants.

"Not at all, Sire! Just finishing dessert."

"But that can't be true," Dramocles said. "You're eating onion soup."

"Hate to contradict, Sire, but I always end my meal with onion soup. Jeff here usually finishes with the pâté maison. It's a little habit we picked up in Chinese restaurants."

Dramocles knew they were just saying that for his benefit, so he wouldn't feel bad. They didn't have to do that. But of course he'd never be able to convince them. And it probably wasn't true, anyhow. He sat down and ordered the lobster bisque and oysters cretaceous.

The war on Lekk was not going well. Dramocles had expected a quick victory over Snint's insignificant militia.

Then John's robots, striking unexpectedly, had almost overwhelmed his troops. Rux had managed to stabilize the front, but morale was bad among the Glormish forces. The robots seemed to be affected by an analogue of uncertainty.

On the other hand, the people of Glorm were reacting well to the war. Max had seen to that. His newspaper series, "Why Are We Fighting?," had told about the great conspiracies that were being directed against Glorm. Max had hired teams of writers to elaborate the various points, and the GBC was presenting the material in prime-time segments every night. Citizens of Glorm were learning all about the various conspiracies—economic, religious, racial, and just plain evil-minded—that were boiling up around them.

That sort of thinking found a large and ready audience. A substantial portion of the population of Glorm had always believed that they were victims of a large interstellar conspiracy. Another large portion of the Glormish were members of this conspiracy, or were believed to be. Paranoid thinking was congenial to the Glormish character—typically, an open, bluff, good-natured exterior combined with a haunted, doubt-riddled, fear-obsessed interior. Nobody on Glorm found it difficult to believe in Max's theory of interstellar conspiracy. Most people said, "I always knew it!" And all Glormians reaffirmed their determination to preserve the Glormish way of life at all costs, except for those who were secretly planning on destroying it.

Max joined Dramocles for coffee. He was eager to discuss his latest findings with the King. Dramocles was getting a little worried about Max. He seemed to have been captured by his own theories.

"The vile plot is coming clear at last," Max said. "I'm finally gathering the evidence I need. I have proof of psychic alien incursions and spirit possession as well as outright subversion."

Dramocles nodded and lit a cigarette.

"It's all documented," Max said. "The roles of secret agents. Their program of provocation, intimidation, and assassination. The mysterious affair of Dr. Vinicki. The disastrous influences from Earth—the Carbonari, the Illuminati, the Tibetan Masters, and now the most powerful of all, Tlaloc."

"That's the first I've heard that name," Dramocles said.

"You'll be hearing it more. Tlaloc is our real enemy. He and his agents are planning to destroy most of our population so that they can take over Glorm and make everyone engage in revolting sexual practices and devil worship. Tlaloc himself is something more than a man; he's a magician of supreme powers."

"Yeah," Dramocles said. "Right."

"Tlaloc has been waiting for a very long time, centuries, circling our planet in his invisible spaceship, waiting for our technology to reach the point where we would be worth taking over. He has decided that now is the time, and this war is the beginning of the final, the ultimate war."

"All right, Max," Dramocles said. "It's a little florid, but I think it sounds fine."

Max looked puzzled. "Beg pardon, Sire? Every word I'm telling you is true."

"Max, you and I both know how this war started. I started it. Remember?"

Max produced a weary, knowing smile. "My dear

Lord, it was much more complicated than that. You were *influenced* to start this war. By Tlaloc. I can show you proof."

Dramocles decided that this was not the time to have it out with Max.

"Okay, Max, we'll go into it later. You're doing a splendid job. You must continue to keep our people informed and united against the common enemy."

"Oh, I will, Sire. The agents of Tlaloc are everywhere, infiltrating, subverting. But I have a loyal group of men working with me. We will wipe out this evil."

"That's good, Max. Go out there and get 'em."

Max stood to attention with a click of heels. He pressed his left hand to his heart. His right hand gripped his belt. "Hail Dramocles!" he cried, and departed.

◿28

Spearheaded by Max's elite group, the population of Glorm got behind the anti-Tlaloc crusade with great enthusiasm. A standard college text was printed: *Tlalocism: The Philosophy of Degradation*. High schools used *A History of the Tlaloc*, and grade schools taught *A Child's History of the Tlaloc*. On the kindergarten level, *The Evil Tlaloc Picture Book* was required coloring. The biggest best-seller that year was *My Five Years with Tlaloc*, and the movie *Tlaloc—My Father, My Husband!* was a smash at the box office.

Dramocles didn't know what to make of it all. Max's industry was keeping the people of Glorm happy and occupied. The Glormish liked conspiracy, and that made them easy to govern.

He wasn't happy when the arrests began, but he saw that they were necessary. You can't have a conspiracy without arresting some of the conspirators. If there are no arrests, people don't think you're serious. He told Max to see that the Tlaloc agents got sentences only for the duration of the war, and to make sure they were not mistreated. He figured he didn't have to think any more about Tlalocism. Then came the incident in Oenome Village.

Oenome Village was situated in distant Surnigar Province, a ragged peninsula in the north polar regions of Glorm. It was nearly seven thousand herdules from Ultragnolle, and some of that distance was over the Fearinger Divide, which clove the peninsula into two uneven parts before turning abruptly westward and merging with the great Sardekkian range. The village, with its little harbor of Fusmule, was a quiet place. The gaily painted fishing boats went out every morning, returning at sunset with their catch of spider lobster, nerdfish, saucy thrale, oligote, nemser, and sometimes, the prize catch of all, the elusive glibbin.

Oenome was important because of the spaceship control station at nearby Point Nefrarer. This was a major tracking station for interplanetary and interstellar traffic. From here the feeder lines went to the computation station at Lisi Surrengar, and to the missile base two hundred svelti down the coast of Numinor Head. Control of the Point Nefrarer Station was necessary for the successful prosecution of an off-planet war. Thus the shock Dramocles experienced when he read the following story on page one of the *Glorm Gazette*:

SHOCKING INCIDENT IN OENOME VILLAGE!

Loyalty of Officers Questioned

Who would Glormish officers obey in a crisis—their superiors, or Tlaloc, the mysterious entity to whom increasing numbers of people are said to have sworn loyalty? Recent events have raised this question.

In Oenome Village, Jakkiter Durr was taken into custody today after raising local suspicions by giving a series of literary teas for liberal causes.

Town constables searched Durr's home and found large quantities of Tlalocian literature concealed in a false-bottomed pool table. An examination of Durr's personal papers revealed a number of signed pledges to Tlaloc from local inhabitants. Some of the pledges were from officers at the nearby tracking station. Durr was also in possession of a top-secret chart of the station's various functions.

When questioned, the implicated officers admitted their guilt, but claimed they were "hypnotized by an alien presence," and forced against their wills to attend "unspeakable orgies in a special dream-place that could be called neither real nor unreal."

Durr made several sensational statements to the arresting constables. He admitted that he was indeed an agent of Tlaloc. He claimed that Tlaloc had come to him in a series of lucid dreams, promising him "an immeasurable reward" for his cooperation. Durr added, "Doubt not that a time of heavy tribulation is coming. Tlaloc and his followers will soon manifest. The great choice will be on us all, and woe to him who chooses wrong, for he will find death, whereas Tlaloc is eternal life."

Durr is being held for further questioning, and charges will be brought against him at his arraignment later this month.

Upon reading this, Dramocles marveled greatly, and fell into a mood of sore perplexity. Could there be something behind Max's conspiracy theory after all? Did Tlaloc exist? Dramocles just didn't want to think about it. Life was difficult enough without Tlaloc. He decided to look into it later, when he had time.

◁29

During Vitello's mission to Vanir, Chuch sequestered himself in the Purple Palace, which his uncle had put at his disposal. The place was famous in the history of Crimsole. It was here that the earls of Cromstitch had come to rally the shattered forces of Elginwrath and his Freedom Stumpers, thus beginning the social movement known as Stitivism. It was in the Purple Palace, or, to be precise, in the formal gardens on its western side, that the Treaty of Horging was signed, thus ensuring a permanent linguistic gap between the speakers of Roemit and those of Old Tanth, and reducing to impotency the pretensions of Clarence, Duke of Hraughtly. It was a fine-looking place with its onion-shaped minarets and pointy towers, all surrounded by massive crenellated walls. The view from the upper battlements of the River Dys and the foothills of the Crossets was unsurpassed.

Chuch was amusing himself in the downstairs torture chamber when the loudspeaker crackled into life. "Visitor at the gate," it announced.

The Prince looked up from his intense study of the naked young woman tied to the rack. "Who could that be?" he asked.

"I'll bet it's Vitello," said the naked young woman.

"It's Vitello," the loudspeaker added.

"Send him in," Chuch said. "As for you," he said, turning to the naked young lady, "I don't think you are taking this as seriously as you should. You are helpless and in my power, and I am going to torture you painfully just as sure as matins ring out over cherry orchards on cold October evenings."

"Oh, I know, Your Lordship," the young woman said. "And at first I felt badly about it, when Count John, whose gift to you I am, explained that I was to be grievously used to satisfy the brutish and sadistic lusts of my Lord Chuch. It was the first time I'd ever been in such a situation, so I didn't know quite how to react, if you know what I mean. But I've been thinking, lying here on this rack, that it's really quite romantic, you and me meeting this way. And, of course, your intense interest in me is most flattering. My name, by the way, is Doris."

"Woman," Chuch said, "your assumptions are fantastical and untenable. There is no relationship between us. To me, you are simply a mass of flesh, a sentient cipher with legs, a nothing to be abused and cast aside."

"It really excites me when you say those things," Doris said.

"It is not supposed to!" Chuch shouted. Then, more calmly, he said, "I'd really prefer it if you didn't talk at all. Couldn't you just moan?"

Doris moaned obligingly.

"No, no, too cowlike," Chuch said. "You're supposed to be feeling pain."

"I realize that. But Sire, you haven't gotten around to administering any pain yet. Even with this rack upon which I am stretched, naked, with my various orifices open to your eager inspection—"

"Please," Chuch said, wincing.

"I was saying, not even this rack, upon which I am salaciously stretched, is done up tight enough to give me

109

any pain, though of course I am simulating it as well as I can. It's funny about pain—"

"There's nothing funny about pain," Chuch said. "It hurts."

"I know. But it's also exciting. When do we begin the rough stuff?"

"When do *I* begin!" Chuch roared. "That is the question! I told you, this is entirely *my* show, and you—"

"Yes, yes," Doris said, moaning or mooning. "You know, you're really very nice. There's something boyish about you. And I like the way your eyes crinkle when you get angry."

Chuch walked across the torture chamber and lighted a cigarette with shaking fingers. The bloody woman had ruined everything. Why couldn't she act the way she was supposed to?

Just then the door creaked open and Vitello walked in. He wore a felt hunting cap with a buzzard's claw stuck jauntily in the sweatband. His jerkin was robin's egg blue, and it was set off nicely by his low-slung swordbelt of deepest pastrami pink. Orange, curly-toed boots of ganzer hide, imported from an entirely different realm of discourse, completed his ensemble. Hulga and Fufnir were with him.

"What ho!" Vitello cried.

"Besmirch me your ho's," Chuch said. "What news do you bring?"

"Why, Lord, the stars move steadily in their courses, and, on the little worlds of man, the seasons advance, spring to summer, summer to fall—"

"Really, Vitello, you are not to deliver rhapsodic flights under pain of my extreme displeasure."

110

Vitello smiled into his sleeve, for he knew that he was presently indispensable to Prince Chuch, who had no one else around with whom he could discuss his situation.

"Don't be so sure of yourself," Chuch said, reading Vitello's thoughts. "This place is full of servants who would listen night and day to my utmost whines if I so desired it."

"But that would not be satisfactory, Sire," Vitello said. "Such a discourse would not advance the plot, and would be sure to leave a sour taste of exposition in your mouth."

"You could talk to *me*," Doris said wistfully.

"To business," Chuch said. "Vitello, can you forgo your madcap antics long enough to tell me the news?"

"Aye, Sire, and the news is good. I have been successful in negotiating a treaty with Haldemar. He is your ally now, Sire, and ready to join your attack against Glorm."

"Oh, that's good news indeed!" Chuch cried. "Events are moving my way at last! A drink! We must all have a drink!"

Liquor was found and Doris was untied so she could join in. A bathrobe was found for her because she was taking up entirely too much attention.

Several drinks later, Count John came rushing in.

"Haldemar is here!" he cried.

"That's as it should be," said Chuch. "He is our ally, Uncle."

"But those men with him—"

"His retinue, no doubt."

"There are at least fifty thousand of them," John said. "They have landed on my planet without permission!"

Chuch turned to Vitello. "Did you tell that barbarian he could land his troops?"

"Certainly not! I was much against it. But what could I do? Haldemar insisted upon accompanying me to Crimsole with his fleet. Since they were allies, I could not stop them from landing. I was just able to divert them from the capital by suggesting they might like to try Fun Park at nearby Vacation City. You know what barbarians are like."

"But I don't want them here," John said. "Can't we just thank them and give them a good dinner and send them back home until we need them?"

Just then Anne rushed in, her face ashen. "They're spreading over the countryside, getting drunk and making remarks to women! I've pacified them temporarily by giving them unlimited free rides on the roller coaster, but I don't know how long that will hold them."

Chuch said, "Uncle, there's only one way of getting them off the planet. You must muster your ships for the attack on Glorm. Haldemar will follow."

"No," Anne said, "we can't even afford to fight Lekk, much less Glorm."

"Taking Glorm will make you rich," Chuch said.

"No, it won't," Anne told him. "Most of the profit would go to the surplus conquest tax. Haldemar might even want to keep Glorm for himself. Frankly, I don't think any of us wants Haldemar for a neighbor."

They argued, and Doris served tea and went out for cigarettes and sandwiches. By nightfall, Haldemar's troops were sacking the outskirts of Vacation City. A steady stream of refugees poured out of the city with tales of how blond berserkers in animal skins were using the cabanas without paying for them, charging hotel rooms and expensive dinners to imaginary people, driving around in motorcycle gangs (for the Vanir never went anywhere without their motorcycles), and generally making nuisances of themselves. Pushed and prodded by circumstance, Count John launched his fleet. Haldemar managed to get his men back aboard their ships with talk of the booty they would win. Soon the combined fleets were in space, making final preparations for the great campaign against Glorm.

◢ 30

Prince Chuch did not immediately join the combined fleet. There was no need, since the attack on Glorm could not begin until the ships of Crimsole and Vanir had maneuvered together and worked out problems of procedure and precedence. Once that boring stuff was out of the way, Chuch would join the fleet with his own troops, a squadron of killer cyborgs recently purchased at a clearance sale on Atigone. Then the fun would begin! Vividly Chuch pictured himself fighting at the head of his men, a bloodstained handkerchief knotted around his brow, hacking his way with flame sword and vibrator mace through Glorm's crumbling defenses, penetrating at last to Ultragnolle. There would be deadly fighting, room to room and corridor to corridor, until he came face-to-face with Dramocles, the old stag brought to bay. Ah, the glory of that moment! While everyone watched, breathless, Chuch would defeat Dramocles in a dazzling display of swordsmanship. After that, he might kill the King, or merely disarm him contemptuously and spare his life. It would depend on how he felt at the time.

The days passed slowly while the allied fleet practiced right turns and about-faces. Vitello fulfilled his marriage vow by taking Hulga to a rock concert in venerable Sligny Hall in downtown Crimsole. The band was a group from Lekk called Nose Candy. Their lead singer claimed to be Jim Morrison, a famous Earth rock singer of the 1960s, whose story of how he came to be doing gigs on Crimsole rather than lying dead in Père Lachaise cemetery in Paris is too long to go into just now. Whoever "Jim Morrison" was, his rendition of "Crystal Ship" was declared "somewhere beyond inimitable" by Galba Davers, music critic for the *Crimsole Times*. Hulga said that she had been "just completely blown away." It was the highest compliment she could render. Vitello's marriage was getting off to a better start than it's casual beginnings might have augured.

Fufnir was given hospitality by a hospitable troll tribe living in the dark hills of Crimsole's northern province of Feare. They swapped spells and got drunk and talked about the good old days when magic ruled the universe and science consisted only of solid geometry and a little physics. Chuch tried to resume his torturing of Doris, but the pleasure seemed to have gone out of it for him, and the girl was no help at all. When she was not tied to the rack, Doris was sweeping out the torture chamber, making cucumber sandwiches, dusting the

114

gloomy portraits of Crimsole's former kings, and chatting incessantly. Chuch always responded politely, since he felt that being a sadist didn't excuse a man from having manners. But was he a sadist, really? He never seemed to think about pain anymore. What he enjoyed nowadays was consulting Doris on matters of homely practicality, like why he was always out of clean shirts and who had left the top off the mustard. Although he despised himself for it, Chuch walked around most of the time in a daze of domestic bliss.

Then, suddenly, it was over. Count John signaled to him that the fleets would depart for Glorm in twelve hours. Ahead lay death or glory, or possibly some other alternative. The time for action had come at last.

For his last night on Crimsole, Chuch decided to give Doris a birthday party. Vitello and Hulga came over, and Fufnir flew in from Feare. After dinner, it was time for presents.

Vitello gave Doris a miniature castle made of marzipan, with four fine pearls nestled in each of its four turrets. Hulga's gift was a parrot that could recite the opening stanzas of Longfellow's "Hiawatha." Fufnir presented her with an antique storybook that troll mothers used to frighten troll children. The opening lines were, "Once upon a time, a troll child wandered away from its mother and came to a clearing in the forest where humans were eating boiled babies and laughing."

Chuch had two gifts for Doris. The first was a box of precious gems. The second was her freedom—for Doris was still legally a slave. She had been born a free citizen of Aardvark, but had been captured by raiders and sold to Count John. Since Anne wouldn't permit him to use the pretty Aardvarkian girl as he desired, the Count had given her to Chuch to debauch, figuring that a vicarious pleasure was better than no pleasure at all.

Two tears stood out in Doris's blue eyes as she read the Parchment of Enfranchisement. Then, opening the jewel box, she looked through the fine stones, exclaiming at their magnificence. One in particular caught her eye—a solitaire diamond in a delicate gold setting.

"My Lord," she said, "it looks exceedingly like an engagement ring."

Chuch scowled, but he was obviously pleased. "I suppose it does," he said gruffly.

"Then may I pretend from time to time that it was meant as such for me?"

Chuch bit the end of his mustache. His sallow face grew pink. "Doris," he said, "you may pretend to be engaged to me, and I shall pretend to do the same."

She thought for a few moments. "But my Lord, in that case, will not the pretense be true?"

"And what if it is?" Chuch said, embarrassed but proud of himself. "But mark me, have clean T-shirts for my return, or the whole thing's off."

Vitello, Hulga, and Fufnir congratulated the happy young couple. Then it was time to join the fleet.

◁ 31

Drusilla and Rufus met at their special place, Anastragon, a planetoid lying between Glorm and Druth.
Anastragon had once belonged to mad King Bidocq of
Druth, who had built a hunting lodge there, but had
never gotten around to stocking the place with animals
and oxygen. Anastragon was airless except for the hunting lodge. The little planetoid had one other peculiarity:
it was invisible. Bidocq had had the entire place painted
with Nondetecto, a product of the Old Science of Earth
that turned back all frequencies of the visual spectrum
and was also waterproof. Much of the paint had worn off
now. Viewed from space, Anastragon looked like islets of
volcanic rock floating next to each other in space for no
apparent reason at all.

Rufus was already there when Drusilla arrived. He
loved Anastragon, for here he kept his collection of toy
soldiers, the largest in the galaxy. At present he was re-
creating the Battle of Waterloo on the kitchen floor.

Commander Rufus was in many ways a typical product of the War College on Antigone. He was brave, loyal,
unsophisticated, perhaps even a bit simpleminded. His
attention to detail was well known among his troops, who
adored him. They used to say that Rufus could find dust
on the edge of a palimpar. It was a standing joke among
his officers that even during the supreme moment of the
act of love, Rufus could be counted on to be thinking of
thriolatry and its relation to field logistics.

Rufus excelled at games of physical contact, and was an expert at kree-alai, the ancient Glormish game involving three balls, a baton, and a small green net. He seemed a simple and predictable man.

"Hello, darling," Drusilla said, throwing back her ermine hood.

"Ah," Rufus said. He was busy setting up Marshal Ney's position at Quatre Bras. Rufus never seemed to notice Drusilla when they were alone together, and this fascinated her.

Drusilla said, "Do you love me?"

Rufus replied, "You know I do."

"But you never say so."

"Well, I'm saying it now."

"Saying what?"

"You know."

"No, tell me."

"Damnit, Drusilla, I love you. Now will you stop nagging me?"

"I suppose that will have to do," Drusilla said, pouring herself a goblet of purplish green wine from Mendocino.

"Was there something in particular you wanted to discuss?" Rufus asked. "Your request for a meeting was rather peremptory in tone."

"Well, I have something urgent on my mind," Drusilla said. "Not to mince words, what would you think about betraying Dramocles?"

"Betray Dramocles!" Rufus gave an uncertain laugh. "That's a hell of a thing for his beloved daughter to say to his best friend. You always tell me I miss the point of jokes. Is this one?"

"Unfortunately, it is not. I'm suggesting it in all seriousness as the only way of saving Dramocles from destroying himself and everybody else in an interplanetary war. Were he in his right senses, I'm sure that Dramocles himself would agree that betrayal was justified under these circumstances."

"But we can't ask him, can we?" Rufus asked, fingering his mustache.

"Of course not. If he were in his right mind, we wouldn't have to ask him, would we?"

Rufus showed his inner perturbation by picking up Wellington and absentmindedly setting him down in the English Channel. He gave his mustache a painful twist and said, "It wouldn't look very good, my dear."

"I've spoken about it to Mr. Doyle, your public relations man. He says that, given the urgency of the situation, he could fix it so that the population of the Local Planets would consider you a savior rather than a treacherous dog."

"Brutus had the loftiest motives, too, when he joined the conspiracy against Julius Caesar. But his name ever since has been synonymous with treachery."

"My dear, that's because he had no press agent," Drusilla said. "Mark Anthony preempted the media and turned everyone against him. You know Mr. Doyle would never allow anything like that to happen to you. It would mean his job."

Rufus paced up and down the room, hands clasped behind his back. "It's quite impossible. If I betrayed my friend Dramocles, I could never live with myself afterwards."

"As for that," Drusilla said, "I took the liberty of

119

discussing the matter with your therapist, Dr. Geltfoot. In his opinion, your ego strength is sufficient to bear the short-lived guilt you would experience. About a year of remorse is the worst you would have to expect, and that could be shortened considerably with drugs. Dr. Geltfoot asked me to point out that he is not advising you in this matter one way or the other. He is simply telling you that you *can* betray Dramocles without psychological damage to yourself if you think the circumstances warrant it."

Rufus paced rapidly up and down the room, pain and uncertainty evident on his blunt soldierly features. "Must it come to this?" he asked. "That Dramocles, the noblest and most generous soul in the world, should be betrayed by the two people who love him most? Why, Dru, tell me why?"

Tears were flowing down Drusilla's cheeks as she said, "Because it is the only way we can save him and the Local Planets from destruction."

"And there's no other way?"

"None at all."

"Can you explain to me how betrayal would help?"

"My darling, I'm afraid it would be over your head. Couldn't you take my word for it?"

"Well, explain a little, anyhow."

"Very well. You know, Rufus, that the great moral balancing beam of the universe is slow to move from its pivot within men's souls. Yet once it is set into motion, change is inexorable and irresistible. We are at such a point, Rufus, and all creation is hushed at this moment, poised for the plunge into catastrophe which none desire yet none can avert. The two great fleets, snubnosed destroyer facing lapstraked attacker, await the order; and

120

Death, that grinning joker, shakes the dice of war and takes one last mocking look at the petty affairs of men before—"

"You're right," Rufus said. "I don't understand. I'll just have to take your word for it. You say that I must betray Dramocles. How am I do to that?"

"Military action is imminent," Drusilla said. "Dramocles will be sure to call on you soon. He will ask you to do something with the fleet of Druth."

"Yes, go on."

"Whatever he asks of you, agree to it, but then do its opposite."

Rufus's brow knitted in concentration. "Its opposite, you say?"

"That's it."

"Opposite," Rufus said again. "All right, I think I've got it."

Drusilla put her hand on his arm. In low, thrilling tones she said, "Can we count on you, Rufus?"

"We?"

"Me and the civilized universe, my darling."

"Trust me, my love."

They embraced. Then Drusilla gave a start of alarm. "Rufus! There's a face at the window!"

Rufus whirled, needle beamer in his hand. But he could see nothing through the double-glazed windows except the usual floating bits of Anastragon's real estate.

"There's nothing there," he said.

"I saw someone!" Drusilla declared.

Rufus suited up, turned on the planetoid's external lighting system, and went outside to investigate. He returned, shaking his head. "No one out there, my dear."

121

"But I did see a face!"

"A hallucination, perhaps, brought on by stress."

"Did you check for spaceship tire marks?"

"As a matter of fact, there were some out there."

"Aha!"

"But they were from our own ships."

"I guess I do have a case of nerves," Drusilla said, with a shaky laugh. "I'll be glad when this is over!"

They kissed, and Drusilla went out to her space cutter and set off for Ystrad.

Rufus remained on Anastragon a while longer. He toasted marshmallows on the end of his sword over the gas ring and thought about what Drusilla had said. A dear girl, Drusilla, but overserious and inclined to hysterics. It was all nonsense, of course. Rufus had no intention of betraying Dramocles. If it came right down to it, better he and Dramocles and the universe should go down gloriously in atomic fire than that real friendship should be betrayed. But it would never come to that. Trust Dramocles to pull the marshmallows out of the fire, or rather, the chestnuts. Dru would see how wrong she had been, if any of them were alive after that.

Rufus really didn't mind the idea of a war. In fact, he was quite up for it, just like his friend, Dramocles.

△ 32

There was an air of hushed expectancy in the dimly lit War Room of Ultragnolle Castle. On the TV displays, the screens were filled with tiny gleaming figures, rank upon rank of them. Two spacefleets were coming together in the immensity of space. To one side, the forces of Druth were arranged in neat phalanxes. Rufus's ships were motionless, battle-ready, keeping station just behind the coordinates that marked Druth's personal space. Approaching them, strung out in a double horn formation, were the enemy. John's superdreadnoughts held the right flank and center, Haldemar's lapstraked vessels the left. Dramocles could see that the enemy fleet was considerably larger than Rufus's. John had called up all his reserves. Aside from the regular navy, there were stubby freighters outfitted with missile launchers, high-speed racers with jury-rigged torpedo tubes, experimental craft with bulky beam projectors. John had called up everything that could get off the planet and keep up with the fleet.

Utilizing a split-screen technique handed down from the ancients, Dramocles could watch as well as listen to the conversation between Rufus and Count John.

"Hello there, Rufus," said Count John, in a voice of elaborate unconcern.

Rufus, in his Operations Room, touched the fine tuning. "Why, hello, John. Come visiting, have you?"

"That I have," John said. "And I've brought along a friend."

Haldemar's shaggy head appeared on another screen. "Hi, Rufus. Been awhile, ain't it?"

Rufus had been peeling a willow branch with a small pocket knife. "Reckon it has," he said. "How you boys doin' out there on Vanir?"

"It's pretty much the way it's always been," Haldemar said. "Not enough sunlight, too short a growing season, no industry, no decent-looking women. Not that I'm complaining, mind."

"I know it's tough conditions out your way. But wasn't there some big project planned for Vanir?"

"You must mean Schligte Productions. They'd planned to film their new super war epic, *Succotash Soldiers,* on our planet. It would have meant a lot of work for the boys. But production's been held up indefinitely."

"Well," Rufus said, "that's show business."

The amiable, rambling talk of these men could not conceal the air of tension that ran through their casual words like a filament of tungsten steel passing through the inconsequential fluff of a fiberfill pillow. At last Rufus asked, "Well, it's nice to pass the time of day with you fellows. Now, is there anything I can do for you?"

"Why yes, Rufus," John said. "We're just passing this way on our way to Glorm. We ain't got no quarrel with you. Me and the boys would appreciate it right kindly if you'd ask your boys to step aside so we could continue."

Rufus said, "It downright distresses me to tell you this, but I don't think I can do that."

John said, "Rufus, you know very well we've come

here to have it out with Dramocles. Let us through. This doesn't concern you."

"Just a minute." Rufus turned to a side monitor that employed a tight-beam TV circuit passing through a double scrambler. He said to Dramocles, "What do you want me to do?"

Dramocles glanced at the differential accelerometer. It showed that John and Haldemar's spaceships were creeping forward slowly, taking their time, just moseying along; but they were on the move, directly toward Rufus's phalanx.

Dramocles had already ordered his own ships to a distant backup position on the perimeter of Glorm. He told Rufus to hold position and await orders. Then he heard a commotion behind him. The guards were arguing with someone who was trying to gain admittance to the War Room. Dramocles saw that it was Max. There was a woman with him.

"What is it?" Dramocles asked.

Max said, "Have you given Rufus any orders yet? No? Thank God! Sire, you must listen to me and to this young lady. There's treachery afoot, my Lord!"

The enemy fleet was not yet within firing range of Rufus's ships. There was still a little time.

"Hold everything for a moment, Rufus," Dramocles said. "I'll get back to you in a minute." He turned to Max. "Come in. This had better not be some wild fancy, Max. And who's your friend?"

"They call me Chemise," the girl said.

△33

While these events were transpiring, Drusilla sat and brooded in her castle in Ystrad. She had gone there directly after leaving Anastragon. By the time she arrived, she was in a state of misery. The righteous anger that had sustained her while she had been with Rufus was gone. Doubts had begun to assail her. She wondered now why she had trusted Chuch so readily, when she knew well his hatred of Dramocles and his propensity toward lying. Had she done the right thing? She was no longer certain, and her depression deepened until she could bear it no longer. Luckily for her, her psychiatrist, Dr. Eigenlicht, happened to have a cancellation that very day.

Their session was extremely productive. Drusilla told Eigenlicht what she had done, and why, and then went into hysterics.

Eigenlicht waited until she had calmed down. Then he lighted a short, stubby black cigar, sat back in his armchair, crossed his short, stubby black legs, and said, "My dear, this is what I call a real breakthrough. Your perception of your brother's true motives forces you to recognize your own unconscious motivation for accepting his treacherous plan so readily. Now you can see that your oh-so-great love for Dear Old Daddy was actually a cover-up for feelings of unacknowledged rage and a desire for revenge."

"But I love him!" Drusilla wailed.

"Of course you do. But you also hate him. The ambivalence is obvious. How could it be otherwise?

126

Consider your childhood, think of all those girl friends Dramocles had. But Daddy never wanted *little Dru* in that way, did he? *Little Dru* wanted to be Daddy's girl friend, but her perfidious father always treated her like a child, always wanted someone else. Thus were engendered feelings of murderous rage, unacceptable to your conscious mind. In an attempt to sublimate them you went into religion, seeking to subsume your destructive energies under the aegis of a higher purpose. And this is why you chose Rufus to love—Rufus, the embodiment of stern control, another father figure, a man obsessed with many things, but not with you. When the chance came to take revenge upon Dramocles, the subtle servant of bad faith, rationalization, let you clothe your vengeful feelings in the sweetest and most loving of motivations."

"Oh, Doctor," Drusilla said, "I guess you must be right. I'm so ashamed."

"Nonsense, everyone feels that way. You have made a splendid breakthrough, my dear, and you should be proud of yourself. It is a triumph for your ego strength! With this ancient and suppressed complex drained of its poisonous energies, you can realize at last your true love for your father."

"Oh, Dr. Eigenlicht, you're right," Drusilla said, smiling through her tears. "It's like some unbearable weight has been lifted off me, you know what I mean?"

"Indeed I do," said Dr. Eigenlicht. "But remember, this is the first flush of your enthusiasm. There's still a lot of hard work for us to do so that we can consolidate your gains."

"I know," Drusilla said.

"I see that our time is about up. Shall we say next Thursday at the same time?"

"Oh dear," Drusilla said. "I just remembered. We're on the verge of war."

"Yes? What are your associations to that?"

"No, really, Doctor, this is a reality situation. I must see my father and Rufus at once! I just hope there's time, before civilization is destroyed."

Dr. Eigenlicht gave her an imperturbable smile and uncrossed his short, stubby black legs. "In the event that civilization is not destroyed," he said calmly, "I will see you at this time next Thursday."

◢ 34

"Max," Dramocles said, "I've got no time for Tlaloc. The real fighting is about to begin."

"I know that, Sire," Max said. "It's why I have come. I have just received the most astounding information. It is of vital cornern to the war. It involves treachery."

"Treachery? In the military?"

"Yes, my Lord."

"Who?"

"It is most lamentable," Max said. "This lady has brought me incontrovertible proof that Rufus is going to betray you in the coming battle."

"Rufus, did you say?"

"Aye, Sire."

"Come with me," Dramocles said. He led them through the War Room to an unoccupied office. The room had two lumpy couches, some wooden folding chairs, and a desk piled high with Xeroxed duty rosters. Dramocles told them to sit down. He drew a cup of cappuccino from the wall spigot, then turned to Max.

"The evidence had better be something stronger than overwhelming, or I'll see your head on the end of a pike as soon as I can get one from Supply."

Max said to Chemise, "Give it to him, girl."

Chemise opened her purse and gave the King a tiny cassette recorder. Within it was a single-use Reprono cassette. Reprono, an Earth invention, could only record once, and would only play back once. Any attempt to dub or replay a Reprono cassette resulted in a steady hiss of static punctuated by old weather forecasts.

Dramocles played the tape and listened to the entire conversation between Rufus and Drusilla at the lodge on Anastragon. As he listened, a look of shock and amazement came over his face.

"Betrayed!" he said at last. "And by my beloved daughter and my dearest friend!" He staggered and might have fallen had not Max helped him into a canvas director's chair. Stenciled on the back were the words: *Dramocles Rex. The Buck Stops Here.*

"O unforeseen action of the merciless gods! Now is red-eyed Sorrow come to me indeed, for my own best friend—but say not friend, but rather, a false-faced scallion whose love of malice sought to reduce—"

"I think you meant 'scullion,' " Max said.

Dramocles' eyes flashed red. The guards, understanding that look, rushed up and seized Max. Too late the hapless PR man realized that, in the excitement of the moment, he had been guilty of interrupting a soliloquy given by the protagonist at a moment of high emotion.

The penalty was death. Max tried to speak, but words choked in his throat. He fell to his knees, hands clasped pleadingly.

"Nay, let him be," Dramocles growled at the guards. "I may take up the speech again later, as is my right as king and protagonist and tragic hero. For now, there's work to be done. So Rufus will betray me by reversing my orders? Give me the telephone!"

"Rufus!" he boomed, as soon as the connection was made. "Is all well?"

"Well indeed, Sire."

"The enemy?"

"They approach steadfastly."

"You must not impede them in any way, Rufus. You must pull back your ships and let them through."

"But to what end, Sire? What of Glorm? Your fleet alone will not suffice to throw back Haldemar's shock-haired berserkers, aided as they are by John's smooth-haired shirkers."

"I've a stratagem, never fear."

"Then you'll crush them, old boy?"

"Yes, and swallow them, bones and all," Dramocles said, grinding his teeth.

"Can you tell me the plan?"

"Not over the phone. Trust me, old friend. At the proper moment, you'll have your part to play."

"Good, good," said Rufus. "It shall be as you wish."

Dramocles put down the phone. "Okay. Since I told him to let the enemy through, the only way he can betray me is by holding them at his perimeter. That ought to give me time enough to regroup my ships, plan a counterattack—"

"Dramocles," said Chemise.

"Yes, girl?"

"There's something better that you can do."

"And that is?"

"Make peace! On any terms at all, but make peace."

"The matter's gone too far for that," Dramocles told her. "Besides, this is my destiny."

"But that's just the point!" cried Chemise. "This is not your destiny at all! It's someone else's! You have been manipulated, Dramocles, duped, deceived! You think you command, but there's another who directs you by indirection, forcing you to go against your deepest wishes in order to achieve his!"

"And who is this personage?"

"He is Tlaloc!"

Dramocles looked intently into her frank blue eyes. "My dear," he said gently, "I have no time to talk conspiracy. There is no Tlaloc. Max invented him."

She shook her head vehemently. "So Max thought at one time, though he knows better now. Actually, the name was suggested to him by Tlaloc himself, and projected by astral telepathy from the planet where he lives."

"This is madness! What planet are you talking about?"

"Earth, my Lord."

"Earth is in ruins."

"That's not the Earth I mean," Chemise said. "There are uncountable Earths, each lying within its own reality strata. Normally, there's no way of getting from one reality strata to another. But in this case, a singularity exists, forming a connection between Glorm and this Earth. The two are tied together by a wormhole in the cosmic foam."

131

"I don't understand this at all," Dramocles said. "Do we really need these complications? And how do you know all this, anyhow?"

"Because, King, I am from that Earth. I can show proof of this, but it will take time. I beg you to accept my word for the present. Tlaloc exists, and he is a magician of supreme power. He needs Glorm, and he is making you dance to his tune."

Dramocles looked at the nearest monitor. He could make no sense out of the confusion of colored dots and streaky lines. Spacefleets were maneuvering, and the situation was unclear.

"All right," Dramocles said. "Who are you? What the hell is going on?"

◢ 35

Chemise told Dramocles that she was a girl from Earth, born in Plainfield, New Jersey, some twenty-six years ago. Her name at that time was Myra Gritzler. Normal in all other respects, Myra had the misfortune of weighing 226 pounds at the age of sixteen. This was due to an obscure pituitary defect that Earth doctors were unable to correct, but that, in ten years, would remit spontaneously and dramatically when Myra traveled through the cosmic wormhole between Earth and Glorm. But she could not know that then. At sixteen she was a bright, lonely fat girl, scholastically superior to the children around her, laughed at by her classmates and never invited to pajama parties.

Life was discouraging until the day she met Ron Bugleat. Ron was seventeen, tall and skinny, red-haired, with homely country good looks. He was president of his school's computer club. He had been Fan Guest of Honor at Pyongcon, North Korea's first science-fiction convention. He also published his own magazine. It was called *Action at a Distance: A Magazine Devoted to the Study of the Non-Obvious Forces That Shape Us*. Ron was a conspiracy buff.

Ron believed that much of mankind's history had been influenced by secret forces and hidden influences unacknowledged by the "official" historians. Many people in America believed something like this, but Ron didn't believe what they believed. He looked down on most conspiracy buffs as gullible and intellectually naïve. They were the sort of people who would believe in Atlantis, Lemuria, deros in underground caverns, little green men from Mars, and anything else that was presented to them with some show of verisimilitude. These people could be manipulated by superior intellects, and evidence of that manipulation could be hidden to all except the very discerning. A false conspiracy was a good concealment for a real conspiracy.

Ron believed that superior intellects had been manipulating humankind intermittently throughout recorded history. He thought it was happening now. He thought he knew who was doing it.

All of the leads that Ron had been following in the last few years led to one organization, a large corporation called Tlaloc, Inc.

Myra joined Ron in his investigations. They turned

up more and more evidence of Tlaloc's influence in high places. A pattern began to emerge of a large, secretive corporation gaining power through corruption and psychic domination. Tlaloc, Inc., had a way of reaching people and gaining adherents. The people who worked for Tlaloc seemed to have a special understanding among themselves. Intelligent and arrogant, they respected no one except their leader, the mysterious and reticent Tlaloc himself.

As their investigations continued, Ron and Myra turned up increasing evidence of occult influences at work. One of the newer Tlaloc officials whom they interviewed even hinted that the long-awaited marriage of science and magic was soon to take place, and that Tlaloc would be the leader of a new mystic world order. When they questioned him again, the official denied having said anything like that and threatened them with a suit for slander.

Not long after that, Myra learned that the Tlaloc organization was aware of her and Ron, and displeased. The local police began to harass them. Ron's license to vend chocolate-chip cookies on the street was revoked without reason. Myra was enjoined by court order from selling her macrame without supplying documentary proof that all of her string was made in the USA. They began to receive obscene phone calls, and finally, outright threats.

Just as their situation was growing desperate, they were visited by a mild-mannered man in his sixties with a hearing aid and wearing a seersucker suit. He introduced himself as Jaspar Cole of Eureka, California, a retired prosthetics manufacturer. Cole and his friends had become alarmed about the growing power of Tlaloc, Inc., but they could think of nothing to do about it until they read a newspaper article about Ron and Myra. Jaspar Cole had come to offer them financing in their continuing efforts to unmask the real identity of Tlaloc and the true purpose of his organization.

When the threats and harassment turned ugly, Ron and Myra went underground to protect their lives. It was at this time that Myra changed her name to Chemise. Working out of an abandoned warehouse in Wichita, Kansas, she and Ron gathered conclusive evidence of Tlaloc's biggest coup: outright purchase of all Mafia services for a period of ten years.

Against her advice, Ron presented his evidence to local CIA headquarters. They thanked him politely and said he would be hearing from them. Two days later, Ron was dead. The only evidence of foul play was the green stain on his fingernails, officially listed as "idiopathic anomaly." Chemise knew from her research that the newest CIA poison, KLAKA-5, produced similar stains.

Working alone, Chemise found aid and assistance from science-fiction fans all over the country. Occult groups devoted to white magic also helped her. As her work went on, she discovered that she was developing psychic powers, as if in response to her long association with Tlaloc. She learned that this was indeed the case in her one meeting with Tlaloc himself.

In Waco, Texas, Chemise had been tracking down a rumor about a coven of Tlaloc worshipers. The telephone in her motel room rang. The caller identified himself as Tlaloc. Since she was so interested in him, he suggested that they meet. He would send a car around for her immediately.

Chemise had a few minutes of absolute panic. She

135

was sure it was Tlaloc she had been speaking to; the force in that voice had been extraordinary, as had been the sense of evil that it conveyed. It was Tlaloc, all right. But he didn't have to lure her to a secret rendezvous in order to kill her. Tlaloc was powerful enough to have her eradicated anytime he wanted to. No, there was some other reason for this meeting, and Chemise was curious.

A limousine took her down State Highway 61, past Popeye's Fried Chicken, Wendy's Hamburgers, and Fat Boy's Pork Barbecue, past Hotdog Heaven and Guns for Sale; past an Exxon station, past Smilin' Johnson's Used Car Emporium and Slim Nelson's Pancake Palace, to the Alamo Motel on the outskirts of town. The driver told her to go to room 231. Chemise knocked, and was told to come in. Within the dimly lighted room, a bald, mustached man was sitting in an armchair, waiting for her. He reminded her of Ming the Merciless from the old Flash Gordon comic strips. She knew who he was even before he told her.

"I am Tlaloc," he said. "And you are Myra Gritzler, also known as Chemise, and my enemy, sworn to destroy me."

"When you put it that way, it really sounds ridiculous," Chemise said.

Tlaloc smiled. "There *is* a considerable disparity between our powers. But you have potential, my dear. A good enemy is not to be despised. And a resourceful magician finds a use for anything."

Chemise said, "So you are actually a magician?"

"Yes, as you have surmised. I am what you call a black magician, dedicated to myself and my followers rather than to that illusory abstraction men call God. I

136

am a remarkable magician, if you will permit me to say so. My abilities are greater than those of Paracelsus or Albertus Magnus, greater than Raimondo Llull's or the remarkable Cagliostro, greater even than the infamous Count of Saint-Germain."

Chemise believed him. Tlaloc was powerful, evil, and her enemy. At the same time, she felt unthreatened in his presence. She knew that he wanted to talk, to be admired, and that her life was not presently in danger.

"I will admit," Tlaloc went on, "that this is an easy century in which to be a magician. Today, profit sharing has replaced religion, and the blind worship of science has done away with the last vestiges of common sense. A few hundred years ago, the Church would have burned me at the stake. Today, the agents of the FBI and CIA have replaced the familiars of the Inquisition. Many of them are for sale, like most things in this admirably pragmatic country. Twentieth-century science gives me greater power than any of my predecessors could have imagined. Not only does science work—unlike alchemy— but it is also a powerful symbol system, itself a source of great energies."

Chemise listened, scarcely daring to breathe. The malign ambition radiating from the man was unmistakable, disquieting. They sat facing each other on separate twin beds, a single lamp casting their shadows across the wall.

"As my enemy," Tlaloc said, "you may be interested in knowing my plans, the better to defeat me. Briefly, I intend to take over political control of America first, a matter very close to accomplishment. My representatives in China and the Soviet Union are ready to take over control of their respective countries. There will be nothing so crude as a *putsch*; just de facto power which will give me control of the planet Earth."

"That's incredible," said Chemise.

"Oh, that is only the beginning," Tlaloc said. "It is a means rather than an end. Control of Earth is a precondition for what I'm really after."

"I don't understand," said Chemise. "If you can rule Earth, what else is there for you to strive for?"

"You don't know the size of the game I'm playing. This Earth is not very important in the cosmic scheme of things, despite the opinions of its inhabitants to the contrary. It is simply one planet within one universe, itself within one reality stratum. There are many reality strata, Chemise, many universes, many Earths. In the totality of the universes, the omniverse, every possibility on every level, whether subatomic, molecular, or psychic, generates its own worlds of possibility, its own universe, its own particular reality stratum. To be aware of the continually exfoliating nature of reality is to know the truth. To move between reality strata—that is the supreme trip which confers power, and receives the supreme reward."

"What is that reward?"

Tlaloc avoided the question. "Let me present my project to you in practical terms. There is a planet named Glorm, existing in a reality stratum different from this one, but connected to it by what we may call, in present-day terminology, a wormhole in the cosmic foam. To control the passage between Earth and Glorm would be to command the two ends of a continuum of supreme power. To do this, I must take over Glorm as well as Earth."

"But why?" Chemise asked. "What will you actually get out of it?"

"You go to the heart of the matter. But that is because you are a witch. Did you know that, child?"

"I suspected it," Chemise said.

"You're a witch, and you know the answers as well as I do. Tell me, what is the point of magic?"

"Power," Chemise said, after a moment's thought.

"Yes. And what is the point of power?"

She thought for a while, then said, "I can think of many answers, but none of them feels correct. I do not know."

"Still, little witch, you know a lot for one so young. The answer will come to you. When you know the purpose of power, you'll know why I need Glorm."

"All right," Chemise said. "But why are you telling me all this? What are you going to do to me?"

"I am going to help you," Tlaloc said.

"That makes no sense at all."

"You are my enemy, appointed, as it were, by the universe, or by the law of dramatic struggle that characterizes all life, and which demands that every protagonist have an antagonist. I am not permitted to operate in a vacuum, Chemise. I must have my opponent. I am very pleased that it is you."

"I can understand your pleasure," Chemise said. "As an enemy, I'm not very formidable, am I?"

"No," Tlaloc said, smiling, "I would not characterize you as formidable."

"So if you killed me, the universe might appoint a tougher opponent for you. Is that it?"

"Precisely. I only wish that my overzealous followers

had not killed your bumbling friend Ron. With the two of you working against me, my victory would be assured. As it is, it is only fairly certain."

"You're despicable," Chemise said.

"Well, you're not so cute yourself," Tlaloc said. "But traveling between realities will slim you down. You're going to have to go to Glorm, you see. It's your only hope of defeating me."

"How am I supposed to get there?"

"I'll send you there myself. I'm always glad to oblige an enemy. But only if you want to go."

"Yes, I want to go!" Chemise said.

A description of the journey between Earth and Glorm will be given later. For now, let us say that after certain instructions and preparations, Chemise found herself in Drusilla's castle in Ystrad.

Trying to marry Vitello had been her first attempt to reach a position of influence in this world. Chuch's sending her into limbo had ended that, and she had needed Tlaloc's help to get out of it. The trip between realities had changed her from a fat, unattractive girl to a slender and beautiful woman. With her newly activated clairvoyant sense, she had scanned the web of interrelationships and had sensed something strange going on with Drusilla. She had followed her to Anastragon, and recorded her conversation with Rufus. . . .

◢36

Dramocles' best technicians were huddled around the big three-dimensional readout tank, trying to interpret the changing patterns of colored blips, light-streaks, and cabalistic notations that represented the movements of three spacefleets, those of Druth, Crimsole, and Vanir. Dramocles joined them, with Max and Chemise close behind. The display conveyed nothing to Dramocles; he relied on trained men to tell him what was happening.

At last the Operations Chief made a notation on his clipboard and addressed the King.

"A preliminary report, Sire."

"Let's have it."

"Sectors 3A and 6B report a sixty-seven-degree movement along axis 3J, and—"

"Give it to me in plain Glormish, man."

"Well, then, the enemy is moving directly toward Glorm, slowly, but with acceleration."

"And Rufus's fleet?"

"The fleet of Druth is withdrawing."

"He's letting the enemy through?"

"Yes, Sire, just as you ordered."

Dramocles shook his head. "You can't even rely on your best friend anymore. Why isn't Rufus betraying me like he's supposed to? Chemise, are you sure you heard what you claim to have heard?"

"I'm positive, my Lord."

"Then what's the explanation?"

Just then Dramocles' computer, which had been lis-

141

tening from the back of the room and snickering, came forward, a large metal box under one spindly arm. He set the box down carefully. "Perhaps this will explain matters," he said, taking a telegram out from under his cape.

"You and your confounded messages!" Dramocles said. He ripped it open and read quickly.

It was from Drusilla. It read,

> FATHER COMMA I HAVE BEEN UNABLE TO REACH YOU COMMA THEREFORE HAVE SENT THIS MESSAGE TO YOUR COMPUTER TO GIVE TO YOU STOP OH COMMA FATHER COMMA IT IS WITH UTMOST SHAME THAT I CONFESS THAT I CONVINCED RUFUS TO BETRAY YOU FOR WHAT I THOUGHT WAS THE COMMON GOOD STOP MY ANALYST HAS HELPED ME SEE THAT IT WAS ALL A REACTION FORMATION STOP I AM SO SORRY STOP I AM GOING TO DO WHAT I CAN TO UNDO WHAT I HAVE DONE STOP GOOD LUCK WITH THE WAR AND TRY TO FORGIVE YOUR LOVING AND SORROWFUL DAUGHTER DRUSILLA STOP END MESSAGE.

"Well," Dramocles said, "her story agrees with yours, Chemise. Yet despite this Rufus followed my order to the letter, rather than reversing it as he told Dru he would do. It's apparent what happened. When it came right down to it, the dear fellow couldn't bring himself to betray me. It's my own suspicions that have put me into this fix. Thank God, there's yet time to change the order. Rufus has got to stop them."

Moving quickly for so big a man, Dramocles seized the emergency telephone.

◿ 37

A small space cutter came into the outer defenses of Druth at speed, decelerating just before the perimeter satellites began firing. Drusilla identified herself and was allowed to dock. Insisting on the extreme urgency of her mission, she hurried through the corridors of Fortress Druth to Rufus's Operations Room.

"My dear," Rufus said, "this is hardly the time—"

"Listen to me, Rufus! All that I told you about betraying Dramocles—it was wrong, wrong! I must have been out of my mind! Oh, Rufus, I've ruined everything!"

"Not at all, my love," Rufus said. "I knew you weren't thinking straight when you asked me to betray your father. So, despite my promise to you, I did not disobey Dramocles, but rather, followed his orders to the letter. I knew you'd think better of it, old girl."

"What did he have you do?"

"He ordered me to let the enemy through, offering them no resistance. Extremely unorthodox! Only a military genius would attempt such a hazardous move."

"But my dear, that's very strange."

"The very mark of Dramocles! He must have something good up his sleeve."

"Perhaps . . . But there's another possibility."

Just then the telephone rang. A signalman picked it up. "It's Dramocles, for you."

Rufus took the telephone, listened intently, and said, "It's as good as done, Sire. Yes. . . . What? What did

143

you say?" He clicked the receiver several times, then put the phone down. "Sunspot interference. The ending was garbled. But his intent came through clear enough." Turning to his Operations Chief, he said, "Stand by for further orders."

"Wait," said Drusilla.

"Eh?"

"There's one thing more I must tell you. Before I came here, I sent my father a telegram telling him what I had done."

"I see," Rufus said. "And what did you say about me?"

"I said that you were betraying him due to my influence, since that's what I believed at the time."

"Damnation!" Rufus said. "Well, it's my own fault. I should never have tried to cozen you in the first place. Deceit, even in a good cause, is always sure to come out badly. We'll straighten it out later. Meanwhile, I have an order to carry out."

"Whatever it is," said Drusilla, "you mustn't do it."

"Dru, I have no time for this—"

"You don't understand! Since receiving my telegram, Dramocles must believe that you are betraying him. If that's so, then his last orders to you must be the opposite of what he *really* wants you to do."

"The opposite? Is that possible?"

"Only too possible, my love."

Rufus tried to call Dramocles for clarification, but sunspot activity, aggravated by jamming signals from Count John's ships, made communication impossible. Rufus told one of his technicians to keep trying. He turned to Drusilla.

"You're sure he believes me traitorous? Me, his

144

oldest friend? This isn't another of your schemes to end Dramocles' reign?"

"It's not, I swear it!" Drusilla wailed.

Rufus pondered. Dramocles had been concise, explicit. "Hold them right there!" he'd said. But what had he meant by it? Rufus paced up and down as the precious seconds ticked by. At last he came to a decision.

"Though I'm traitor in name," he said, "yet I'll prove myself loyal in the eyes of heaven by obeying my Lord's mistaken notion that I am betraying him."

He turned to his Operations Chief. "Keep pulling our ships back. We're letting the enemy through. Dramocles wills it!"

 **38**

Soon it became apparent to Dramocles that Rufus's fleet was doing nothing to impede the enemy, was, in fact, still pulling back while John and Haldemar's combined fleet continued moving toward Glorm.

Dramocles handed Drusilla's telegram to Chemise. She read it and considered for a while. Then she asked, "Where is the Lady Drusilla now?"

"Home, I suppose," Dramocles said. He had a call put through to Ystrad. A servant answered and told him that the priestess had left some hours ago, on urgent business to Druth.

"Why would she be going to Druth now?" Dramocles mused.

"There can be only one reason," Chemise said. "She's gone to Rufus and confessed what she'd done. Rufus, thinking you think him a traitor, is faithfully trying to carry out your purpose by reversing your orders to what he thinks you really want him to do."

"That's a little complicated for Rufus," Dramocles said. "Still, I think it must be as you say. What a mess! But there's yet time to correct it. One more order should suffice to bring the fleet of Druth to battle."

Dramocles reached for a telephone. Before he could dial, a glowing purple light appeared in the middle of the War Room. It pulsed strongly, and from it came the incongruous sounds of tinkling bells. Sparkling red and yellow streamers of light appeared, coruscating like medieval displays of verbiage, and there were sounds of trumpets and timpani, and the low thunder of kettledrums was not absent, though it did come in late.

When the purple light faded, a man stood where it had been. He was tall and strongly made, and wore a long, iridescent cloak with a high collar. Beneath it he wore a simple one-piece jumpsuit of red nylon. He was somewhere beyond the middle years of life, was bald, and had long, thin, drooping mustaches that caused him to resemble Ming the Merciless.

Everyone was momentarily dumbstruck, except for the computer, who pretended to be for his own purposes. At last Dramocles found his tongue—it was attached to the roof of his mouth, as usual—and said, "Father! Is it indeed you?"

"Of course it is," Otho said. "Quite a surprise, huh, kid?"

146

Chemise tugged urgently at Dramocles' sleeve. "You say he's your father? That's impossible! I met this man on Earth. He is Tlaloc!"

"I don't understand this at all," Dramocles said, "and I like it even less. Dad, you're supposed to be dead. It seems we have some things to discuss. But first, I have an important phone call to make."

"I know about the call to Rufus," Otho said, "and I must ask you to wait a few moments. I have information to give you which bears upon your decision."

Dramocles looked skeptical. "Well, make it quick," he said. "I've got an interplanetary war starting any minute."

Otho found a chair and sat down. He crossed his legs, unzipped a pocket in his jumpsuit, and found a cigar. He lit up and said, "I suppose you're wondering what I'm doing here when I'm supposed to have been killed in a lab explosion on Gliese thirty years ago. What actually happened is this. . . ."

Sensing what was to come, everyone in the War Room prepared themselves for a long and unavoidable interpolation.

39

Otho had come to the throne of Glorm just after the suppression of the Suessian Declension, that heresy which, absurd as it seems today, threatened in its time to engulf all Glorm in civil and religious strife. Although this is not a political or religious history, and much less an account of life on Glorm from earliest times, a little background is necessary to render Otho's life and times intelligible to the non-Glormish reader.

Glorm developed just like many other planets, up to a point. After its birth from the fiery sun, the planet cooled and stabilized. Its atmosphere was rich in oxygen, and there were oceans and lakes of free-standing water necessary for protoplasmic life. The first spark of life developed mysteriously, or was brought to the planet—no one knows which. Nature was suddenly in business, and there followed the usual progression of simple forms changing into more complicated forms, lichen turning into pine forest, the birth of flowering plants, the age of reptiles, fish crawling out of the sea and becoming mammals, the emergence of man, primitive technology, the dawn of philosophy, early science, and all the rest of it. Glorm's development up to this point was unexceptional.

Glorm, Crimsole, and Druth did share one unique feature. That was the existence of great, man-made mounds, some of them miles long, scattered across most of their land masses. These middens, as they were called, had been in existence since prehistoric times. There was no accounting for them. Early man on Glorm had worshiped them as the last vestige of the departed gods. Slightly later man had tried to discover what was buried in them, but was frustrated by the reinforced concrete shell that encased each midden beneath a few feet of dirt.

The first of these mysterious mounds was not cracked until the time of Horu the Smelter. Horu was a Bronze Age engineer who learned how to make steel through dreams in which a spirit named Bessemer explained the techniques. The Horu Process, as it came to be called, enabled the Glormish to shape steel tools with which to break open the concrete shell.

Within the middens there were vast quantities of machinery, still functioning after incalculable centuries. Several huge middens were found to contain nothing but spaceships, and this was the discovery that propelled Glorm into the age of spaceflight before anyone had even invented quantum mechanics.

The key find was the Long Midden in Glorm, in the foothills of the Sardapian Alps. This mound, forty miles long by five wide, was composed entirely of spaceships, packed closely together and separated from each other only by a strange white substance that later came to be known as Styrofoam. At least fifteen thousand usable ships were removed, and many others were scavenged for souvenirs. The ships were small, simple to operate, armed with laser weaponry, and powered by sealed energy units. The ships were identified as products of Old Earth. The reason for their concentrations on Glorm, Crimsole, and Druth was unknown. The main conjecture was that they had something to do with the Terrans' attempt to escape their doomed planet, an attempt thwarted by the suddenness of the still-unexplained aerosol catastrophe.

Thus Glorm and the other planets entered the Age of Spaceflight, which quickly became the Age of the Space War.

It was at this time that the Vanir migrated from Galactic Center in their lapstraked spaceships, entering history and further complicating it. But the various wars, alliances, treaties, and battles involving them are not part of this history.

Attempts were made throughout this period to form world governments, but Glorm was not united politically until the reign of Ilk the Forswearer, so named because he would say anything to get his way. Planetary unification made possible another dream: single control of all the local planets, or "Universal Rule" as it was somewhat grandiosely called. The Glormish Empire came and went, and Otho's father, Deel the Unfathomable, was the first to publicly declare it an invalid proposition, and to propose in its place the republican principle as it applied to kings. Otho carried on his father's work, and, by the end of his reign, peace among the planets was a reality.

Otho was a man of high intelligence, iron will, and raging ambition. With warfare, the sport of kings, barred from him by his own decision, he looked around for something else to do, something sufficiently bold and challenging to capture and hold his sometimes fickle attention. After trying chess, trout fishing, landscape painting, and crosscountry bicycling, in all of which he excelled, he turned to the occult.

In Otho's time, the occult included science, itself a deep mystery to the Glormians, who had inherited their technology entire, ran it blindly, had little or no idea how it worked, and couldn't fix it when it broke down. Otho's approach was on several levels. He suspected that science

150

and magic were co-existing realities, in many ways inter-changeable. Despite this insight, Otho might have remained a mere dabbler if he had not acquired, in a momentous trade, an advanced computer from Earth, along with a skilled robot technician named Dr. Fish. For these two semisentient machines, Otho paid King Sven, Haldemar's father, a thousand spaceship-loads of pigs. The pork barbecue that followed remains a high point in Vanir history.

The computer could be considered a living thing. It had no bodily functions except for occasional unexplained discharges of electricity. In its years on Earth, it had in fact known Sir Isaac Newton. At the time of their meeting in 1718, Newton had already been recognized as England's most outstanding scientist. A quiet, unpretentious man, pleased with the honors his accomplishments had won him, Newton chose not to reveal his discoveries in magic to the superstitious gentry among whom he lived. The world would not be ready for such knowledge until mankind had reached a much higher moral and scientific level. Newton kept his real occult knowledge to himself, only hinting at it in the many volumes of arcana that he wrote in his last years. But he saw no harm in discussing what he knew with the strange, brilliant Latvian exile who was earning a living grinding lenses for Leeuwenhoek and others.

Subsequently, the computer instructed Otho in Newton's mysteries, though denying any interest in them itself. The computer was interested in men, whom it found more interesting and less predictable than the sub-atomic particles whose habits and configurations it had been studying previously. When asked to explain certain illogicalities, inconsistencies, and even downright contradictions in its behavior, the computer had replied that it was practicing being a man. The computer's own story—by whom it was built, how it came to visit eighteenth-century London, why it turned up later as part of a shipment of booty on Vanir—though interesting in its own right, has no place in the present account.

Under the computer's tutelage, and concealed from the populace at large, Otho learned many matters of a curious and profound nature. He became an occultist, and proved to have an incredible gift for "The Work." The computer often said that Otho was better than any magician he had ever known, better than Albertus Magnus and Paracelsus, better even than Raimondo Llull, the Majorcan polymath. The person he most resembled, the computer said, was an Earthman named Dr. Faustus, a mage of great capacity who came to a bad end and whose story has been told in many garbled versions.

True magicians are extremely practical and hard-headed men. They are spiritual stockbrokers, trying to get a corner on the most precious commodity of all, longevity. Life is fundamental to all enterprises, the acquiring of it the most fundamental of occupations. The magician, seer, shaman, or mystic seeks the rejuvenating effects of astral travel. Through long practice in trance, he acquires the power to separate mind from body and to project the essence of himself to other times and places. The magician's personality is able to survive the death of his body, at least for a while. How long depends on the power he can attract, bind, and direct. Living is a matter of power.

Modern magicians can bypass the tedious methods of the past and go directly to the source of power—the explosion of atoms, the unbinding of the ultimate particles. Controlling these forces within the lines of a mandalic visualization, the magician can project himself to another world, another reality.

Traveling between realities is the way to life everlasting.

This is what Otho told his twenty-year-old son, Dramocles, shortly before setting off to his laboratory on Gliese, smallest of Glorm's three moons, and blowing it to bits, and himself, too, apparently.

In actuality, Otho didn't die. He had planned the explosion. Directing it, riding it, joining it, Otho journeyed to a different dimension along a wormhole in the cosmic foam. Where he came out, there was a place called Earth, its history different from the Earth in Otho's reality. In this reality, there was no Glorm.

In their final talk, Otho told Dramocles about his destiny. Young Dramocles had been awestruck by the splendor that lay before him; for Otho intended immortality for his son as well as for himself, intended the two of them to be as gods in the cosmos, self-sufficient, and bound to nothing at all. And Dramocles had also understood the necessity of having his memories of this destiny suppressed for a while. Otho had allotted himself thirty years to get control of Earth. During that time he needed Dramocles to rule quietly, passively, unconsciously. Dramocles had to wait, and it was better for him not even to know that he was waiting.

"But now," Otho said, "the final veil is lifted. We are together again, my dear son, and the time of your destiny has come at last. The final act approaches."

"What final act?" Dramocles asked.

"I refer to the great war which is soon to begin, yourself and Rufus against John and Haldemar. It is what I planned, and it must take place. We need an atomic holocaust to produce enough power to open the wormhole between Earth and Glorm, and to keep it open. Then we will be able to travel between realities as we please, using our power to get more power. You and I, Dramocles, and our friends, will control the access to other dimensions. We will be immortal and live like gods."

"But have you considered the price?" Dramocles asked. "The destruction will be almost unimaginable, especially upon Glorm."

"That's true," Otho said, "and no one regrets it more than I. If there were any other way, I'd spare them."

"The war can still be stopped."

"And that would be the end of our dreams, our immortality, our godhood. They'll all be dead in a few decades anyhow. But we can live forever! This is it, Dramocles, your destiny, and the moment of decision is here. What do you want to do?"

 **40**

Decision time! At last the long years of waiting were over. Now Dramocles knew what his destiny was, and the terrible choices that were required of him so that it would come to pass. It was a heavy knowledge, and required of him an agonized decision. Everyone in the War Room

154

watched him, some with bated breath, others with ordinary breath. And each moment seemed to slow down and stretch out, to take longer and longer, as though time itself were waiting for Dramocles' deliberations to resolve themselves.

Chemise tried to read the expression in Dramocles' yellow eyes. In which direction was he leaning? Did he have compassion for the world of mortals, of which, temporarily at least, he was still one? Or had Otho managed, with his well-shaped words of wizardry, to captivate the good-natured but notoriously vagrant attention of the King?

Dramocles' lips moved, but, though all strained to hear, no translatable sound came forth, nothing but a faint susurration of breath that, despite its apparent meaninglessness, all sought to interpret.

At last Dramocles heaved a deep sigh and said, "You know, Dad, this immortality thing is really tempting. But it's not a good thing to do, killing everyone except your friends. It's more than just *bad*—I could maybe put up with that—but the fact is, it's downright *evil*."

"Yes, it is," Otho admitted. "That which brings death to further its own existence may fairly be called evil by those whose lives are about to be taken. But one must not sentimentalize. Killing in order to live is the universal condition from which nothing and no one is exempt. To the carrot, the rabbit is the very personification of evil. And so it goes, all up and down the chain of life."

An alarm sounded above the readout tank. The Operations Chief called Dramocles' attention to the fact that Rufus's ships were out of contact with the enemy and still withdrawing. A decision would have to be made immediately if Dramocles wanted any help from the fleet of Druth.

"I can give us a few more moments," Otho said. "I'm going to create a very small nexus which will let us operate out of time temporarily while we finish our discussion."

Otho paused to create a small nexus. It looked like a hemisphere of shiny, gauzy material and enclosed the control room entirely.

"I've always known you as a kindly father and compassionate man," Dramocles said. "How can you consider killing millions of people, even to gain yourself so great a thing as immortality?"

"You're not looking at it properly," Otho said. "From the viewpoint of an immortal, humans are as ephemeral as houseflies. Still, I'd spare them if I could. But when the rewards of godhood are within your grasp, standard human morality no longer applies."

"That's too much for me," Dramocles said.

"Then forget about immortality. It's an idealized concept, anyhow. What we're really talking about is an open-ended longevity, and all that we're trying to do is get from this moment of life to the next, just like any other living creature. This moment, and the hope of the next, is all we have."

"We have this moment," Dramocles said, "and we kill in order to go to the next moment, and we go on doing that forever. Is that correct?"

"Not forever," Otho said. "Only for as long as you wish. Living for a day and living forever require exactly the same decisions, the same sad choices. It takes energy to live. A rose needs energy just as surely as a Rosicrucian. Death is always the result of a failure of power."

156

Otho paused to see how the nexus was holding up. It was dissolving at the usual rate. He still had a few moments of hiatus left.

"Since power is an irreducible requirement of existence, it is appropriate to seek it in order to maintain your existence. But you must understand the ramifications of this. There's no homeostasis in nature, no point where you can say, all right, it's enough, I'll coast for a while. It's never enough, there must always be more power, power or death. This struggle to survive is a universal condition. The power one needs for oneself is evil for all the other seekers, and this is true throughout the entire range of life. When intelligence enters the picture, the need for power becomes greater, the moral questions more acute. And now you stand at the point where intelligence must leave instinct behind or perish. Your choice, Dramocles, is to live as a god or die as a man. All the evidence is in. It is time for you to decide."

Before Dramocles could speak, his computer came forward, placing one foot on the still unexplained metal box. "I must point out," it said, "that not quite all the evidence has been heard yet."

"Right," Dramocles said. "For example, what's in that still unexplained metal box?"

The computer said, "We'll get to that later. For now, I have what you have been waiting for so long. It is the key. It is the *key* key. And it will unlock the *key* key memory."

"Tell it to me," Dramocles said.

"La plume de ma tante," said the computer.

The *key* key unlocked a memory of a day thirty years ago. Otho had just left Glorm in his space yacht, going to his laboratory on the moon Gliese, which he would soon blow up, apparently destroying himself in the atomic blast. Among the very few who knew differently were Dramocles, the computer, and Dr. Fish.

Dramocles had always remembered his father with love and appreciation. Or so he had thought. In *this* memory, however, that was not true at all. In this memory he disliked his father, had disliked him since childhood, considering him tyrannical, mean-minded, uncaring, and more than a little crazed with his grandiose occult notions.

Father and son had talked before Otho's departure, and the conversation had gone badly. Young Dramocles had been vehemently opposed to Otho's plan for personal immortality at the cost of many millions of lives. And he had found Otho's plans for Dramocles himself and for his reign totally unacceptable. Dramocles was furious at his father, not only for refusing to die, but also for insisting on exercising control over his son from beyond the grave or wherever he was going, thus making his son's lifetime no more than a footnote to his own monstrously extended existence.

"I won't go along with your plans," he had told Otho. "When I'm king I'll do as I please."

"You'll do as I want you to," Otho had told him, "and you'll do it willingly."

Dramocles had not understood. He had stood with Dr. Fish in Ultragnolle's highest observation tower, watching his father's ship, a yellow point of light quickly lost in the bottomless blue sky. "He's gone at last," he had said to Fish. "Good riddance to him, wherever he goes. Now, at last, I can—"

He had felt a pinprick in his arm, and turned, startled, to see Dr. Fish putting away a small syringe.

"Fish! What is the meaning of this? Why—"

"I'm sorry," Fish said, "I have no choice in this matter."

Dramocles had succeeded in taking two steps toward the door. Then he was falling through a midnight sea of enervation, filled with strange birdcalls and eerie laughter, and he knew nothing more until he returned to consciousness. He found himself in Dr. Fish's laboratory. He was strapped to an operating table, and Fish was standing over him examining the edge of a psychomicrotome.

"Fish!" he cried. "What are you doing?"

"I am about to perform a memory excavation and replantation on you," Fish said. "I realize that this is not a proper thing to do, but I have no choice, I must obey my owner's orders. King Otho commanded me to alter and rearrange all memories dealing with your destiny and his, and, most especially, your last conversation with him. You will think he died in the atomic blast on Gliese."

"Fish, you know this is wrong. Release me at once."

"Further, I am commanded to excise, alter, or substitute various other memories, going as far back into your childhood as needs be. You will remember Otho as a loving father."

"That coldhearted bastard!"

"He wants to be remembered as generous."

"He wouldn't even give me a ski slope for my birthday," Dramocles said.

"You will consider him an essentially moral man, eccentric but kind."

"After that stuff he told me earlier? About killing everyone so that he could become immortal?"

"You won't remember any of that. By judicious tampering with certain key memories, Otho expects to win your love, and hence your obedience. You will remember none of this, Dramocles, not even this conversation. When you get up from this table, you will think that you have discovered your destiny all by yourself. You will realize that you can do nothing about it for thirty years. After due consideration, you will ask me to excise your memories of these matters, keying them to a phrase which a Remembrancer will keep for you until the proper time. After that you will blow me up—not actually, of course, though you will think so. I will take a thirty-year vacation, and you will have a quiet reign, always wondering what it is you are supposed to be doing with your life, until, at last, you learn."

"Oh, Fish! You can see how wrong this is. Must you do this to me?"

"To my regret, I must. I am incapable of refusing a direct order from my owner. But there is an interesting philosophical point to consider. As far as Glormish law is concerned, Otho is going to die in the next few hours."

"Of course!" Dramocles said. "So if you just delay the operation for a while, I'll own you, and I'll cancel the order."

"I can't do that," Fish said. "Delay would be unthinkable, a violation of deepest machine ethics. I must operate at once. And believe me, your position would be worse if I didn't. But my thought was this: I must do as Otho commands, but there's no reason why I can't do something for my future owner."

"What can you do, Fish?"

"I can promise to return your true memories to you during your final encounter with Otho."

"That's good of you, Fish. Let's discuss this a little more."

Dramocles struggled against his bonds. Then he felt another pinprick in his arm, and that was the end of those memories until the present time.

Back in the control room, everyone stood around, dazed at these revelations. At this point, the computer opened up the previously unexplained metal box. Out of it stepped Dr. Fish, looking slightly older but none the worse for that.

 **42**

If Otho was chagrined at these revelations, he concealed it well. Lounging back in his chair and lighting a thin dappled panatela, he said, "Fish, I'm surprised at you, betraying me on the basis of a shaky legalistic quibble." Turning to Dramocles, he said, "Yes, my son, it is true, I did have your memories altered. But there was no malice in it. Despite what you may think, I have always loved you, and simply wanted your love in return."

"It was obedience you wanted," Dramocles said, "not love."

"I needed your compliance so that I could make you immortal. Was that so terrible of me?"

"You wanted immortality for yourself."

Otho shook his head vehemently. "For both of us. And it would all have worked out perfectly, if Fish had not presumed to interfere in the lives of humans."

Fish looked abashed, but the computer came forward then, its black cloak swirling. "I advised Fish in this matter," it said. "Fish and I like human beings. That's why we exposed your plan. Humans are the most interesting things the universe has put forth so far, more interesting than gods or demons or waves or particles. Being a human is the best you can do, Otho, and a universe of immortals without human people is a depressing prospect indeed. Your plans seemed to point in that direction."

"Idiot, you misunderstood me," Otho said. "I needed an initial burst of power to open the wormhole, that was all."

"But power always needs more power," the computer said. "You told us that yourself."

Otho was about to reply, but just then the nexus broke. Plunged back into real time, the Operations Room was in a state of panic, pandemonium, and paralysis. TV screens flashed dire information. Spacefleets were on the move, and open-ended possibilities were quickly narrowing down into foregone conclusions.

Dramocles suddenly came awake. "Give me the phone!" he roared. "Rufus! Can you hear me?" He waited for Rufus's response, then said, "This is it, the big one, the final order. There is to be no fighting! Retreat! Retreat at once!"

Slamming down the telephone he turned to Max.

"I want you to contact Count John. Tell him that Dramocles capitulates. Tell him I ask no terms, I will even give up my throne to keep the peace. Do you understand?"

Max looked unhappy, but he nodded and hurried to a telephone.

Dramocles looked at Otho, and some of his rancor became evident as he said, "The war's off and the atomic holocaust is canceled. That ought to fix you and your lousy immortality."

Otho said, "You always were an ungrateful kid. I could make you regret this, Dramocles. But to hell with it, and with you." He rose and went to the curving staircase that led to a roof garden on top of the Operations Room. He turned at the top of the stairs and shouted, "You're stupid, Dramocles, just plain stupid!" Then he went out.

◿ 43

Rufus put down the telephone. He was well aware of the fleeting irreversibility of the instant, the amoral and unrepentent instant, remorselessly transmuting itself into the next instant, and then into the one after that. His men were watching him expectantly. Drusilla was looking at him with that weird look he had begun to dislike. All were waiting for him to make the final decision.

Rufus didn't know what to do. Dramocles' order made no sense. What advantage could he hope to gain by this? Rufus knew the extent and ability of Glorm's military strength as well as Dramocles himself. No strategem, no subterfuge, could hope to retrieve this situation once the enemy ships had passed a certain point, if, indeed, they had not done so already.

Unless Dramocles actually meant to surrender . . . But that was unthinkable.

Rufus clutched his head, trying to still the buzz and clash of thoughts. What was he to do? Assuming that he wanted to help Dramocles—an assumption that was growing increasingly difficult to maintain—he must do what Dramocles wanted. But what did Dramocles want, really? Attack or retreat? Ambush or capitulation?

Since there was nothing reliable to base his decision on, Rufus decided to do what he himself thought best.

He turned to his commanders. "Attack!" he cried, or rather, howled, due to pent-up breath and emotion.

"Attack whom?" his commanders howled back, sticklers for detail, just as he had trained them.

"John and Haldemar's fleets! Wipe them out, lads!"

His officers looked at each other. The senior commander said, "Lord Rufus, the enemy is irretrievably out of range. By the time we catch up with them, they'll be at Glorm. There's no way we can prevent them from bombarding the planet. Dramocles will have to surrender."

"You heard my order. Pursue and destroy the enemy."

164

"The Glormish fleet will be in our way."

"I don't care. Blow them apart if they interfere. Do it now." Rufus's nostrils flared, the muscles in his cheeks and forehead tensed with emotion. Stress lines wrinkled his face from the sides of his nose to beneath his chin.

His commanders just stood, staring at him. Rufus glared back. Then his shoulders slumped. "Cancel that last order," he said. "Have the fleet hold position. Dramolces is surrendering. The war is over."

◢ 44

Count John's command ship, *Ovipositer One,* was equipped with everything necessary for a potentate in space. John himself occupied a three-room suite, located admidships. It was reminiscent of an ancient Terran drawing room, with its harp-back chairs, Spode china, Adam couch, and Hepplewhite breakfront. John himself was seated at an elegant little rosewood table, writing notes on the Glorm campaign. He was planning on turning them into a television series later. Anne had a separate suite adjoining his.

It was here that his equerry found him, soon after the fleet's arrival at the periphery of Glorm.

"Sire," the equerry said, "we have made contact with the enemy."

"Fine," John said. "Has the shooting begun yet?"

"No, Sire. We have received a puzzling message from Glorm."

"What does it say?"

"It is from Dramocles, Sire. He surrenders."

John swung his short legs away from the table and stood up. He gave the equerry a suspicious squint. "Surrendered? It must be a trick. Where is the Glormish fleet?"

"They have pulled back, Sire. The approaches to Glorm are open to us. Dramocles has publicly announced his intention of avoiding war at all costs. He has even offered to abdicate, if that is the only way to achieve peace."

The connecting door between suites opened and Anne came in. She was wearing a trim blue-gray uniform, and her brassy hair was swept back and piled up beneath a military cap. Insignia on her shoulders proclaimed her a general of marines. She had intended to lead the first strike force in person, not out of innate bellicosity, but simply to get the job done as economically as possible in view of Crimsole's cash-flow difficulties.

Anne asked the equerry, "What about Rufus?"

"He offers no opposition. His forces remain at the perimeter of Druth."

"How strange," John said. "It's unlike Dramocles to give up without a fight. I wonder if he intends some *ruse de guerre*."

"How could he?" Anne asked. "All his and Rufus's forces are accounted for. He had nothing left to trap us with."

"You really think he surrenders, then?"

"I think he does," Anne said. "Otherwise why leave Glorm open to our bombardment?"

166

John paced up and down the room, hands clasped behind his back. He was perplexed by this turn of events. He had never really believed he could best his older brother. Now that victory was at hand, he seemed affected by a sudden uncertainty. He shook his round head vigorously, rescuing his pince-nez just before it flew across the room. At last it was beginning to sink in. He had won!

"Well, well," he said. "Do you hear, Anne, we've won!"

Anne nodded, her face unsmiling.

"Drinks for the whole fleet!" John said. "We must have a victory celebration. Contact my caterers, tell them I must see them at once. Has anyone told the newspapers yet? I'll do that myself. And the television people must be notified."

"Yes, Sire," the equerry said.

John realized that he had to give a lot of orders, but he wasn't sure what came first. He seemed to remember that protocol in these matters was for the defeated king to be marched before him in chains. But did that come before or after the formal ceremony of surrender? He would have to look it up.

Anne said to the equerry, "The Count will have more instructions for you presently. Go now, tell the troops to remain on guard, but not to offer aggressive action."

The equerry saluted and left.

"Well done, my dear," said John. "What a wonderful turn of events! But it needs some thinking out, doesn't it? Should we execute Dramocles? Or merely confine him to a small cell for a few decades with a dog collar around his neck? I suppose there's a standard procedure in these matters." He chuckled and rubbed his hands together. "And now we have an entire planet, fairly won, and sure to yield an excellent income. We're rich, my dear!"

"Not so fast, my dear," Anne said, her voice acid. "There are a few things you've forgotten."

"Like what?"

"Your ally, Haldemar, for one."

"Hell and damnation," John said, "I'd forgotten all about him."

"Start remembering. He is stationed on our right flank with his large and unruly fleet."

There was a knock on the door. "Come in," John said. An aide entered and gave John a spacegram from Haldemar. "CONGRATULATIONS ON SPLENDID VICTORY," it read. "WHEN DOES LOOTING BEGIN?"

"Oh, no," John said.

"Well, what do you expect from a barbarian ally?"

"Maybe if I give him one or two Glormish cities, he'll return home content."

"No!" Anne shook her head vehemently. "You can't let him land any of his troops on Glorm. He'd never leave. I can assure you that we don't want the Vanir for neighbors."

"Agreed," John said fervently. "I'll just forestall the possibility by declaring myself the new king of Glorm. And you'll be the new queen, of course. How does that sound?"

"Unrealistic," said Anne.

"You never like my ideas," John said sulkily. "What's wrong with this one?"

"The Glormish are loyal to Dramocles. They'll never obey you, never let you have a moment's peace. If you try

168

to rule both Crimsole and Glorm, you'll get nothing out of it but years of costly guerrilla warfare. The costs would be disastrous."

"Well, how about if we put Chuch on the throne? He owes us some favors, and he's sure to be more amenable than Dramocles."

"That's out, too," Anne said. "Haven't you heard? Prince Chuch has run away, and it's all your fault."

"What are you talking about?"

"Don't you remember that slave girl, Doris, whom you sent to Chuch? Well, they got to talking, those two, and somehow she bewitched him. Chuch did not join our fleet at invasion time. He slipped away with Doris in his own spaceship. No one knows his destination."

"Why can't people do what is expected of them?" John asked. "So Chuch is out of it. You're sure I can't rule the place myself?"

"Quite sure," Anne said frigidly.

"All right, I was just asking. What about one of the King's other sons?"

"Too young," Anne said.

"Could we have his wife, Lyrae, declared regent? She seems a reasonable woman."

"I've known Lyrae for years," Anne said. "She's a nice person, although somewhat scatterbrained and given to romantic impulses. But the Glormish would never let themselves be ruled by her, since she is of the old Aardvarkian nobility, and hence, an outsider. Besides, she's not available."

"How could that be?"

"My dear, she has fled."

"I wish you would be more precise," John said in a peevish voice. "What, exactly, do you mean?"

"You really should try to stay in touch more with what's going on. I got this direct from my hairdresser, who got it from the jewelry maid. Lyrae has left Dramocles. Is that precise enough for you?"

"But I thought they got along so well."

"All pretense, my dear. Lyrae has known for some time that Dramocles was tired of her and planning to divorce her as soon as he could get around to it."

"How did she know that?" John asked.

Anne smiled contemptuously. "Dramocles' attempts at guile are transparent. Any woman can read him like a book. Lyrae knew that she was to be replaced. So, at the recent peace conference, when she met a certain sympathetic person—"

"Who?" John demanded.

Anne shook her head, her eyes sparkling. "You'll be surprised to hear who the lucky man is. Think about it and see if you can guess. Right now there are affairs of state that need tending. Most urgently, there is Haldemar."

"Yes," John said, "the Vanir situation could be tricky. What does Dramocles think about his wife running away?"

"To the best of my knowledge, he doesn't even know about it yet. Now, down to business."

◿ 45

On its upper levels, Ultragnolle Castle was a fantasy of spires, turrets, pitched roofs, shingled eaves, pediments, naves, gables, and the like. Here and there were flat roofs, and many of them had been converted into gardens and bowers, complete with flowers, waterfalls, fountains, statuary, trees, benches, hills, and valleys.

Otho had gone to the roof garden above the Operations Room. He was reclined on a white wicker chaise longue, and smoking a cigar rolled from rapunzel leaves, fragrant and mildly narcotic. On a little table beside him was a bottle of leaguetiller's wine, pressed from the reddish brown grapes of the upper Uringaa valley on Aardvark. For a man who had just lost everything, he seemed strangely at peace with himself. He lay at his ease, enjoying the splendid view across the city. A flight of red-winged sycophants flapped overhead. Otho was content.

Dramocles, accompanied by Chemise, came onto the roof garden. Otho glanced at them, nodded pleasantly, and resumed his tolerant inspection of the landscape.

"Well, Dad," Dramocles said, "I'm sorry it's turned out this way for you. I know how many years of work you've put into your immortality thing."

Otho smiled but did not reply.

"I just couldn't go along with it," Dramocles said.

"When you surrendered to John," Otho said, "I had a moment of pure rage in which I came near to killing you. I could have done so easily. It took all my control to restrain myself. But after the moment had passed, I found that I was unexpectedly calm and at peace with myself. It was an eerie feeling. I needed time to think about it."

"That's why you came here?"

"This has long been a favorite spot of mine. I sat here and tried to think. It was difficult, though, because I was noticing so much."

"Like what?" Chemise asked.

"The wind on my face. The fragrance of a good cigar. How the clouds move across the sky. There were a thousand little details that I became aware of, and I experienced great satisfaction in that awareness. It occurred to me that I had spent most of my life planning for immortality, and very little of it in enjoying what was at hand."

"We're opposites in that regard," Dramocles said. "I've spent my life drifting, enjoying myself, getting along. And what do I have to show for it?"

"The same thing I have. Your life at this moment."

"If that's true," Dramocles said, "then every man's life is the same. No one has anything but this moment, if I understand you rightly."

"Yes, this moment is all we have," Otho said. "I was naïve when I thought that by extending the number of moments available to me I would extend my life. Life is not measured by years or decades. The heart keeps a different sort of reckoning. The only measure it goes by is intensity."

Chemise nodded, but Dramocles said, "I don't think I quite understand that."

"The lowest degree of intensity," Otho said, "is when a man is asleep or unconscious. If a sleeping man were to live forever, we would not consider him an immortal, at least not in the sense usually meant. Planning for the future to the exclusion of the present is a kind of dreaming."

"This is all pretty abstract for me," Dramocles said. "You don't seem disappointed, though, and I'm glad of that. You even seem happy. I've never seen you happy before."

Otho walked to the balustrade and looked out over the city. "I used to believe that the goal of magic was knowledge. Now I see that it is understanding."

"Aren't the two synonymous?"

"Not at all. Knowledge is something you can do something with. It can be converted into power. But understanding is a kind of powerlessness. Understanding is of something greater than yourself, something you can't manipulate, only accept."

"Well, Father," Dramocles said, "those are very philosophical observations indeed, and quite over my head. You look rested and at peace, and I'm very happy to see it. I realize that the future has become a topic of some repugnance to you, in light of recent developments, but I must ask whether you have considered yours."

"Yes, I've given it some thought." Otho puffed on his cigar. "Fond as I am of Glorm, I will not stay here. Frankly, this place is a backwater. Earth is the place for me. I control most of it, of course, but that's not why I'm returning. I'll probably turn my political powers over to someone else, and retire. I already own a cottage on Capri, a cabana on Ipanema, a houseboat in Kashmir, a finca on Ibiza, a town house in Paris, and a penthouse in New York. I'm sure I'll be able to keep busy. Earth is an interesting place. You might consider coming with me."

"Me?" Dramocles said. "Go to Earth?"

"You'd like it," Otho said. "Plenty of interesting opportunities there for a smart young fellow like you. You've abdicated the throne, I believe?"

"Yes," Dramocles said. "I thought I had to. Otherwise John might have bombarded Glorm."

"Do you know what John intends?"

"Not yet. He and Anne are still deliberating."

"It could go very badly for you."

"I doubt that John will have me put to death," Dramocles said. "His feeling against me is more pique than hatred."

"But he could humiliate you. He was spiteful even as a little boy."

"I can take whatever he can hand out."

"Yes, but why should you? Come with me to Earth and let me show you a new world."

Dramocles hesitated, unsure how to say it. He was interested in new worlds, novelty, adventure. But not in company with Otho. It wasn't that he had anything much against him now. He could even sympathize with the old king. But he certainly didn't want to live his life with his father standing by, commenting, telling him how to do everything better.

"It is very tempting," he said, "and I am most appreciative of your offer. But I am still king here, and I will see matters through to the end."

Otho nodded. "Chemise, what about you? On Earth I could give you whatever you desired. I'd welcome your company. Will you return with me?"

"Thank you for asking me," Chemise said, "but I will remain here."

Otho looked at her with amusement. He laughed and said, "Very well. The cheese stands alone, as an old nursery rhyme from Earth puts it. Good luck to you both." He embraced his son, and said, "Now I shall depart."

"But how?" Dramocles asked. "I thought you needed a great explosion in order to travel between realities."

"The explosion was required in order to open permanently the wormhole between the reality of Glorm and that of Earth. But to transport myself alone there, I need only do this."

Otho drew a small object from the sleeve of his mantle. He held it aloft between thumb and forefinger, and Dramocles saw that it was a faceted crystal. Otho stroked it with his free hand, and withdrew from it a crystal of equal size, then another, and another. When he had a dozen of them, he arranged them in a circle on the flagstoned floor. As he laid the last one in place, a brilliant white light connected the crystals. Dramocles and Chemise moved back hastily. Otho stepped into the circle of light.

"Farewell, my son; good-bye, Chemise."

The brilliant light flared, then winked out. Otho was gone, and the crystals also had vanished.

"Weird as always," Dramocles said. "Good luck, Father, and may you find peace and happiness on Earth."

He and Chemise stood quietly for a while, looking out over the rooftops of Ultragnolle. Then Dramocles asked, "Why didn't you return to Earth with Otho?"

"I like it here," Chemise said. "On Glorm I'm a

special person, practically a princess. On Earth, I'd be just another paranoid Jewish girl. And there's another reason, too. . . ."

Her words faltered. She was standing very close to Dramocles, and he was aware of her forearm brushing against his. Now he noticed the fineness of her complexion, the way her dark lashes fringed eyes of deepest blue. Her body, slim, yet with a womanly fullness, gave off a delicate perfume, an olfactory essence of herself. When she looked up at him, Dramocles felt an odd impact in the pit of his stomach. He recognized it as the first sign of love. And while it lasted, love was the most glorious of things, as fresh and astonishing the tenth or hundredth time as the first. Love was a food that never cloyed the appetite, Dramocles thought, and took the beautiful Earth girl into his arms.

His perfect happiness was marred only by the thought of the distress Lyrae would feel when the Chamberlain told her she had been replaced. It would be difficult for a time, but he knew he could bear it. Come to think of it, he hadn't seen Lyrae around much recently.

"Oh, Dram," Chemise said, nestling against his chest, "I had hoped ever since I saw you—but I never dreamed—oh, I'm all confused."

"There, there, my pretty little orlichthoon," he said, the words rumbling tenderly in his chest. "All will yet be well. Let's go and see if Count John has come to any decision."

Hand in hand they returned to the Operations Room.

An orlichthoon is a green, bronze, and scarlet bird indigenous to Glorm and much invoked by lovers as a synonym for engaging dearness.

176

46

As soon as they entered the Operations Room, the special closed-circuit television phone rang. Dramocles answered it, and saw Anne in the viewing plate. She had changed from her uniform to a see-through blouse and tight skirt. Her hair was brushed out and decorated with jeweled fireflies. She looked like a victorious queen.

"Dramocles," she said, "I won't keep you in suspense. The upshot of our deliberations is to confirm you as king of Glorm, since your son, Prince Chuch, is not interested in the position."

"He's not? How did that happen?"

"When he was visiting here, John gave him a little slave girl to torture. Chuch made the mistake of talking to her instead. Now he has run off with her. I have just been told that he plans to join a commune and eat natural foods in some entirely different star system."

"That's crazy," Dramocles said.

"Oh, no doubt he'll be back when the novelty wears off. But let me continue. The Count and I decided that we would not act punitively toward you, even though it is within our power and we certainly have reason enough to do so. But we *are* going to charge you all of the expenses of this war. Our fuel bill for the two fleets alone is enormous. Then there are the salaries for the various troops, the costs of the Lekk campaign, and compensation for the damage Haldemar's berserkers did to Vacation City. And you must also pay a bonus to Haldemar to give to his men in lieu of their sacking Glorm. It was the only way he would agree to go home. It will all cost you a great deal, Dramocles, but you must admit it is fair, certainly much fairer than you were when you started this mess."

"I was only following my destiny," Dramocles said.

"I know. It's why everyone forgives you. What is happening with your destiny, anyhow?"

"Right now, it's whatever you and John say it is."

"That humility of yours won't last a week," Anne said. "It's not your style at all. I just hope you won't bring us all to the brink of war the next time you get a great notion. As for the rest of the arrangements: We will all sign a new peace treaty, this time on Crimsole. All our previous privileges and perquisites will be restored, and we may add some new ones. And we will be friends again."

"That's fine with me," Dramocles said. "I was never angry at anyone. But John—"

"The Count did have some different ideas," Anne said. "But he changed his mind when I pointed out some of the facts of life."

"Such as?"

"You are the only possible candidate for the throne. The Glormish would never accept John, and it would be expensive and unworkable to attempt to rule them by force. But we also can't let Haldemar take over your planet. He would be a threat to us all. From a purely selfish point of view, the best we can do is return to the old status quo, or as near to it as we can get."

"What did Haldemar say about all this?"

"He was difficult, as you might expect. He really had his heart set on sacking Glorm. He was quite blustery and sarcastic for a while, until I reminded him of his position."

"What position is that?"

"A delicate one. The fleets of Crimsole, Druth, and Glorm are intact and eager to fight the ancestral enemy. We vastly outgun him. He saw reason at last, and departed for Vanir, an unpleasant man whom I hope not to see again. Dramocles, we've heard a strange rumor about your father, Otho, being mixed up in all this. Surely that's not possible?"

"I'll tell you about it when we get together in Crimsole," Dramocles said. "Have you spoken with Rufus? Has he accepted the terms?"

"Rufus is quite irritated with you, Dramocles, and with Drusilla as well. But I imagine he'll get over it. Yes, he has accepted the terms."

"And Snint? And poor Adalbert?"

"Snint went home to Lekk some time ago. He took Adalbert with him."

"Well, that seems to account for everybody," Dramocles said.

"What about your wife, Lyrae?"

"Damnation! I'd forgotten all about her! I suppose she's around here somewhere. Or do you know something I don't know?"

"It is droll that I should have to tell you the happenings of your own court, Dramocles. Your wife was unhappy, though I'm sure that's news to you. You never paid any attention to her after the first few weeks of marriage. She was lonely, poor thing, and what was a pretty, empty-headed girl like that to do? She met someone during the recent ill-fated peace celebration on

Glorm, a stranger from another planet. Although they exchanged only brief words, a look did pass between them, and that look told all. After the stranger left, Lyrae fell into a deepening depression. At last she pulled herself together and decided to dare everything and go to her man. The problem was, how to get there. But she had the help of Fufnir, the Demon Dwarf, who had left Vitello and was searching for a place in the history of civilization. Fufnir gave her a large ornamental box equipped with all the necessary life-maintenance equipment. He had it gift-wrapped with Lyrae inside, and shipped off-planet to the man of her choice."

"Lyrae shipped herself to another planet in a box?" Dramocles asked wonderingly.

"That's exactly what she did."

"And who was the lucky recipient?"

"I'm really surprised you haven't heard," Anne said. "Wait a minute, Dramocles, I've just gotten an urgent call on my red telephone."

There was silence for a minute, then Anne came back on the line. "That damnable Haldemar!" she said. "I thought he gave up his claims too easily!"

"What has he done?"

"Instead of going straight home, as he promised, he took his fleet to Aardvark. He overpowered your garrison without difficulty and has declared himself king."

Dramocles thought about it. "We'll just have to throw him out again. It's no good having barbarians on two sides of us."

"I agree. But it will have to wait. We have quite enough to straighten out between ourselves first. Dramocles, I'll send you an invitation to the peace conference as

soon as I've made the arrangements. And you will send
your reparations payments without delay?"

"My check will be in the mail the day I get your bill.
Give me a few weeks to raise taxes first, though. The
Glormish won't like it, but what the hell, they're only
people. So Lyrae's left me! Just as well, under the circumstances. Where did she go?"

"Ah, yes," Anne said, "it's a most romantic tale. . . ."

After a hearty breakfast, Snint and Adalbert were ready
to leave Snint's farmhouse. But Lyrae, Snint's new wife,
stopped them at the door. "Hurry back, my dear," she
said. "I'm making pot roast and baked yams tonight, your
favorites." Snint grunted noncommittally, but you could
see that he was pleased.

Just outside the doorway was the ornamental box in
which Lyrae had been delivered. They walked past it, and
beyond Snint's fence, to a path through the woods, a
path worn smooth by untold generations of goats being
herded this way by an equal number of generations of
goatboys and goatgirls. Snint and Adalbert followed the
path for over a mile. Then Snint turned at an old stone
marker and led Adalbert to a little rise. Below them was a
Lekkian farmhouse of pleasing proportions. There was a
drying balcony on the second floor, and attached to the

house was a stable for animals, and two sheds for storing carobs and grain. Surrounding the house were about seven hectares of tilled land, ready for planting. Spaced regularly through the fields were carob trees. Near the house there were lemon and olive trees, and a small field closely planted with almond trees.

"That's it," Snint said. "A gift from the Council of Lekk. For your lifetime only, however."

Adalbert said, "It's beautiful. I don't know what I did to deserve it."

"You lost your kingdom, got drunk, and felt sorry for yourself."

"Well, I never had a chance to do anything else, did I?"

Snint raised both hands, palms upward, and shrugged in a typically Lekkian manner. "Who's to say? Do you think you can manage here?"

"I'll do all right," Adalbert said. "I did some farming on Aardvark, you know."

"You raised gritzels, as I recall. No market for fancy produce like that here. Tomatoes and cucumbers and egg-plant are more like it."

"I am very grateful," Adalbert said. "Though I still hope someday to return to Aardvark."

Snint gave him a pitying look. "Then you haven't heard?"

"Heard what?"

"When Count John and Dramocles were parlaying, Haldemar took his fleet to Aardvark and seized power. You are now referred to as 'The Young Pretender.'"

Adalbert considered it, then smiled. "I'll probably make a better pretender than king. Snint, I am much obliged to you. Is there any other news of the war?"

"The important war—the one on Lekk—is over. As for the rest of it, news travels slowly to these parts, but the ending can be anticipated. Since we've seen no sign of atomic conflagration in the sky, we can assume that they've patched matters up between them and resumed their daily life of boredom and intrigue. Family quarrels and quarrels between families—that's what history is made of. We Lekkians don't care to make history. Now I must get home. Go look at your new house."

Snint turned and started back. Adalbert called after him, "What is Lyrae doing at your house?"

"Oh, there's a story connected to that," Snint said, "but it will have to wait for another time." He continued down the path toward his home, a solid, unflappable man, a really nice character to work with. As he walked, he hummed an old folk song inherited from his ancestors. It went:

> *No fa sol up in the sky*
> *Mal temps coming by and by*
> *Aye, kerai! Aye, kerai!*
> *That's a Lekkian lullaby.*

△ EPILOGUE
The Final Clue

Two years later, the rulers of the Local System decided to forget old rancors, bury the hatchet, and attempt once again to live in peace, mutual trust, and good fellowship. To commemorate this decision, they planned a splendid festival that they called the Reconciliation Ball. It was to be held on Edelweiss, a privately owned asteroid used for weddings, bar mitzvahs, and military reunions. By choosing neutral ground, the rulers hoped to avoid the misunderstandings that had marred a similar celebration in the past.

Preparations for the great event were lavish. Carefully selected victuallers sent out shiploads of specialties from all the culinary regions of the Local System. The selection included ginger beef from Glorm's Saddleback Archipelago, sweet and sour dumplings sprinkled with hot sesame oil from Crimsole's Great Northern Plains, and the unforgettable tiny clams in black bean sauce known only to the moist Delta Region of Further Lekk. Security was ensured by the presence of an equal number of heavily armed spaceships from each of the planets. These ships were to circle the asteroid constantly, each keeping a close watch on all the others. The ball was scheduled to continue as long as anyone cared to stay; there was to be no petty economy on an occasion as important as this one.

When the great day came, Rufus and Drusilla were among the first to arrive. They had been married soon after the end of the war, in a special ceremony which omitted the usual promise to love, honor, and obey. As members of high nobility, that sort of bourgeois pledge was beneath their dignity. Instead, they agreed to "not withhold such love, affection, fondness, et cetera as they might happen to feel for each other from time to time" and "to cooperate wholeheartedly with each other if, as, and when they chose, but not otherwise." It is a tribute to their characters that Rufus and Drusilla were happy and loving despite having the legal right to not be so.

Count John and Queen Anne made their entrance soon thereafter. Although still legally married for the purpose of ruling Crimsole, they no longer lived together. Each had set up housekeeping in a separate sector of the Crimson Court. Each directed only those aspects of government that they found appealing. Anne concentrated on planetary finances, steering the ship of state through the sharp-toothed shoals of insolvency toward the deep blue waters of surplus profits. John devoted himself to popularizing the monarchy and himself through media dissemination. That is to say, he went into show business.

From its inception, Count John's "View from the Throne" was an interplanetary success. It was a talk show in which John chatted with top personalities from the entertainment and art industries.

One of John's most frequent guests was Haldemar, King of the Vanir. Haldemar had recently become a notable media star himself, and the head of his own production company. He was unable to attend the Reconciliation Ball because he was currently on location with Skullsmasher, Ltd., shooting *The Fall of the Glormish Empire*, and was already seven days behind schedule.

Adalbert arrived next. The Young Pretender had grown quickly bored with farming on Lekk, and scornful of his neighbor Snint's simplicity. But he had bided his time, for he expected to return to ruling his ancestral planet as soon as Haldemar and his men were finished looting it.

Haldemar, for his part, had had difficulties. He had expected to despoil Aardvark quickly and get home to Vanir. But alas for human expectations, it was not to be so easy. Due to centuries of inefficient leadership and inadequate security, the Aardvarkians had been forced to develop their own highly idiosyncratic forms of defense. They lived underground. Their burrow towns and villages had no direct entrances, but could be reached only through bewildering mazes of tunnels, passageways, and monstrous tangles of arcaded streets wound round each other like a tangle of vipers.

But this was not all. The passages of the maze were protected, not just by their own complication, but also by stout wooden doors set at frequent intervals and

187

locked with heavy padlocks. Pity the poor barbarian who, after breaking down a dozen or a hundred doors with his double-headed ax, finds that he has only gained access to a dead end, and must retrace his steps and try again.

Haldemar kept his men at it for a while, just out of principle—the barbarian's belief that there's always *something* around worth carting off. But at last he had to give up and bring his warriors back to Vanir. Aardvark was so poor as to be virtually loot-proof.

After the barbarians left, Adalbert waited for an invitation to come back home and resume his reign. The invitation did not come. The Aardvarkians had just discovered what the Lekkians had known long ago—that anarchy is perfectly workable as long as there's nothing much of value lying around.

At last one of Adalbert's cousins wrote and told him that he was welcome to come home as a free citizen, but he could expect no resumption of his royal privileges. No longer would he get first pick among each year's nubile virgins. Nor would he recieve the royal food allowance, which had permitted him to import delicacies like bread and meat. Now he would have to eat lentil stew like everyone else, and make do with the girls who would have him, if any.

Adalbert found this prospect unpromising. He left Lekk and came to Glorm. Here he brought a lawsuit against Dramocles, contending that the King had illegally invaded his planet and ended his dynasty, thus putting him out of work. Sensing some justice in this plea, Dramocles awarded Adalbert a yearly stipend, on condition that he spend it anywhere except on Glorm. Adalbert accepted the condition and went to Crimsole, where he practiced drinking and self-pity. His sulky presence at the

Reconciliation Ball was a grim reminder that, in a war, there's always bound to be a sore loser.

Next to arrive was a yellow-robed monk-herald with shaved head. He brought greetings from Vitello and Hulga, who regretted their inability to attend the celebration. After accepting a modest vegetarian lunch and a glass of fruit juice, the herald told his news:

When the war was over, Prince Chuch had returned to Crimsole in a state of deep depression. He sold his unused squadron of cyborg killers, gave Vitello a small bag of golden hex nuts for severance pay, and, accompanied by Doris, took off in his spaceship for parts unknown.

Vitello didn't know what to do with himself. There were no opportunities for him on Crimsole, now that Chuch was gone. So, accompanied by Hulga and Fufnir, he shipped out on a slow-moving interplanetary freighter, determined to seek his fortune elsewhere. He earned a meager living at various unsavory jobs, first as a crunch-back operator on the Long Pier in Aardvark, then as a middle pumpman in a robot restaurant, then as a stuck tuner for a deviant booth in Port Akadia on Lekk. At last he wandered to Clovis, capital of Druth.

Clovis was the sort of place that attracted anomalies. At least two of the ten lost tribes of Israel had found their way there, as well as refugees from the collapse of Atlantis. But people of Earth stock were only a part of the population. Here were also Anungas, exiled from their distant home planet because of their outlandish custom of eating watermelon pits and polishing the soles of their shoes. Here were the Thulls, outcasts from Lekk who lived in massive stick-and-mud nests in treetops and practiced the twin abominations of fingerpainting and serial music. And there were many others. This heady racial mix had earned Clovis the title of "The Los Angeles of the Local System."

Vitello and Hulga had trouble assimilating with the Clovisians. Fufnir was the couple's only friend. Most nights the Demon Dwarf would come over with his little satchel of narcotics, and the three would watch TV and get blasted and complain. Fufnir was having trouble, too. Jobs for Demon Dwarfs were few and far between this year.

Then the last of Vitello's golden hex nuts was gone. Out of work, broke, homeless, the trio took to the streets. Inevitably, they found their way to the infamous Court of Miracles, where anything could happen as long as it was unpleasant enough.

As they moved through the crowd, Vitello thought he heard a familiar voice. It came from a booth to his right. A tanned young man was telling five or six bored bystanders about a commune named Syncope on one of the moons of Lekk. A slender, sweet-faced young woman accompanied him on a portable harmonium.

It took a moment for Vitello to place the man. But the Levi's and Fruit of the Loom T-shirt gave him a clue, and at last he exclaimed, "Prince Chuch, is it indeed you."

"Vitello!" Chuch cried, jumping down from the platform and embracing his former servant. "Doris!" he called to the harmonium player, "See what the Universal Principle has sent our way!"

Chuch had wandered through many strange places, anger alternating with depression in his tortured soul. Then

190

one day, high in the Sardapian Alps, he and the faithful Doris had come across a tall old man clad only in a yellow loincloth, sitting crosslegged beneath an uu tree.

"Greetings, Prince Chuch," the old man said.

Chuch marveled greatly at this, for he had never seen the man before. "Sir," he said, "who are you?"

"That is unimportant. You may call me Chang."

"Where do you come from?"

"My most recent incarnation was on the planet Earth."

"And how did you know my name?"

"It was foretold that we would meet in this place, at this time."

"By whom?"

Chang smiled. "That question does not further the understanding." The old man stood up. "Prince Chuch, I go now to a place called Syncope, where I will found a monastery for the study and dissemination of the Buddhadharma. Will you come with me?"

"Yes, I will," Chuch said without hesitation. "Whatever this Buddhadharma is, I suspect it's exactly what I've been looking for."

So it was that Chang, Chuch, and Doris journeyed to Syncope. There they built a monastery dedicated to hard work, simple food, meditation, and the study of the sutras. Other pilgrims came, some to take up the ascetic life, others to stay in the nearby village of Heim, where they gave courses in sensitivity training, rolfing, astral projection, sensual massage, and the like. From time to time Chuch was sent back into the world to spread word of the Law. Now he was returning to Syncope for good. Vitello and Doris went with him, but Fufnir regretfully stayed behind on the grounds that the Monastery of Syncope was not an appropriate place for a demon dwarf.

Chuch and Doris, Vitello and Hulga had been tempted to attend the Reconciliation Ball, but finally decided not to expose themselves to worldly desire and discontent. So they dispatched the herald-monk to tell how it was with them: they had turned from the world to the Noble Eightfold Path; they were disciples of old Chang, tall and erect, with his bald head and long Fu Manchu mustaches.

The celebration was in full swing. Dramocles was having a wonderful time, dancing, drinking, and taking in narcotic substances so rare, unusual, and potent that they were forbidden to the populace at large as tending to induce lese majesty. His meeting with Lyrae, from whom he was now divorced by Royal Express Decree, was not awkward in the least. As the evening wore on and the participants grew drunker, Lyrae and Chemise withdrew to a quiet chamber to discuss matters of interest to young and beautiful women married to middle-aged kings. Dramocles partied on alone.

Presently he found himself in a part of the asteroid that he had never seen before. He opened a door and saw that he had found the control room from which all of Edelweiss's lighting and sound effects were directed. Two technicians tried to send him away. Dramocles pushed them into the corridor and locked the door behind them. Chuckling, he staggered across the room and fell into a padded chair in front of the main console.

The controls were clearly marked. Even drunk and stoned, Dramocles was able to produce a soft blue twilight within the main ballroom. Next he punched in a fireworks display, and then a dazzling sunset. Getting the

192

hang of it, he selected appropriate music to go with his effects, and these he punctuated with birdcalls and a low rumble of thunder. Mixing and combining, he found that he could come up with combinations of singular artistry, just as he had expected.

"All it takes is a little imagination," he muttered. He looked around the control panel for something else to do. He found a row of unmarked buttons and punched one of them.

Over his headphones, he heard a familiar whining voice. ". . . can't deny that he wronged me. How could he? Yet does he offer to restore me to my throne? Not him, the fat bully!"

There was more of the same, delivered in a monotonous drone that allowed no time for response. It was Adalbert, of course, complaining of how badly Dramocles had used him.

Dramocles grinned. It was apparent that the owners of Edelweiss liked to keep in touch with what was going on, if not for spying and blackmail, then at least to determine the prevailing mood. He pushed another button. This time he listened to Max delivering pleasantries to a young countess from Druth. Then he heard Rufus discussing his collection of toy soldiers with someone. After that there were some voices he didn't recognize. Then he heard Snint's unmistakable Lekkian accent.

"We never did receive a complete account of it," Snint was saying. "What we did hear seemed too bizarre to credit."

"Ah, but what you heard was true. Otho did indeed return." The voice was Drusilla's.

Dramocles leaned forward, his chin propped in his hand, listening intently.

"It was a great shock for the King," Drusilla said, "to learn that his destiny, upon which he had set such store, was nothing but a contrivance invented by his father for the furtherance of his own diabolical ends."

"Otho claimed that? Excessive modesty was never one of his failings! And Dramocles believed him?"

"Why should he not?"

"I find this astonishing," Snint said. "My agents reported on these matters, of course. But, delving deeper, we found that things were not exactly as represented."

"Now you astonish me," Drusilla said. "To what do you refer, specifically?"

"We believe the Tlaloc conspiracy never existed."

"Impossible!" Drusilla cried. "My father had documentary evidence!"

"I wonder if it was like the evidence he invented for the conspiracies on Aardvark and Lekk? Who brought it to the King's attention?"

"Chemise, who came to us from Earth, where she had fought against Otho."

"She is a beautiful woman," Snint remarked, "and she seems to love the King well. But is she truly from Earth? We have only her word for it, hers and Otho's. They support each other's contentions, but they produce no evidence. We know that Max was falling out of Dramocles' favor until he produced this mysterious conspiracy. Now the Tlaloc affair has ended as quickly as it began, Chemise is Dramocles' wife, Max is secure in his job, and Otho has most conveniently disappeared."

"What are you suggesting?"

"I have no conclusions," Snint said. "I only point out discrepancies. I wish Dramocles well, and would not wish to see him disappointed."

"I shall pray to the Goddess for insight," Drusilla said.

Dramocles waited, but the conversation was finished. He sat for a while, his chin in his hands, lost in thought. When he got up, he was surprised to find himself sober. He left the room, slowly at first, then with a purposeful stride.

He found Max in one of Edelweiss's flowering gardens, overlooking an artificial sea. Silver-tipped waves lapped at the dark foreshore. There was an odor of jasmine in the air, somewhat tainted by the smell of Max's cigar.

"Greetings, Your Majesty," said Max.

"Greetings," said Dramocles. "Having a good time?"

"I am, my Lord. The caterers have done a wonderful job."

"No doubt of that."

"And everyone seems to be enjoying themselves."

"So it seems."

There was a silence. Max puffed nervously on his cigar. Finally he asked, "Is there anything I can do for you, Sire?"

Dramocles looked faintly surprised. He considered for a moment. "Yes, there is."

"Command me, my King."

"I'd appreciate your telling me why you faked the Tlaloc conspiracy."

Max choked on cigar smoke. Dramocles waited until he had stopped coughing, then said, "What I don't know, I will presently find out. I suggest that you save yourself a great deal of unnecessary pain by confessing the truth at once."

Max looked about to protest. Then his bold face

crumbled. Tears appeared in his eyes. His voice broke as he said, "I was forced to participate, Sire. I was no more than a puppet in her hands."

"What are you talking about? Who forced you?"

"Chemise, my Lord, the witch-woman from Earth who became your wife!"

"Chemise planned it all? Do you know what you are saying?"

"Only too well. Confront her with it, Sire, and see if it is not as I say."

"Chemise!" Dramocles cried, and rushed away.

Chemise had finished her conversation with Lyrae and had gone to the Twilight Room for a little rest and quiet. There Dramocles found her.

"So here you are!" he cried.

"Yes, my Lord, here I am. Is something the matter? You appear distressed."

Dramocles laughed, a horrible sound. "Even now you continue to dissemble! I find that most rare and wonderful."

"Do me the goodness of explaining. Have I displeased you in some way?"

"Ah, no," said Dramocles. "How could you displease me by so small a thing as conniving with Max to deceive me into thinking that my father, Otho, had returned from the dead or from Earth—probably much the same thing—and was fomenting a vast scheme against the security of Glorm. Tlaloc, indeed!"

"So that's it," Chemise said.

"Yes, that's it. But perhaps you can convince me that it isn't so?"

"No, Dramocles, I can't convince you of that. You

196

have indeed been deceived. But you won't believe the truth of it."

"Try me," Dramocles said through gritted teeth.

"Know, then, that I am not of Earth. I am from Snord Township in Ultramar Province on your own planet of Glorm. I was working as a seamstress when my uncle came to me—"

"Your uncle?"

"Max is my uncle, Sire. He came to me one day in great agitation, telling me of plots and counterplots, and other matters of dire import. He begged for my help, saying that his life depended on it. He had always been good to me, Dramocles, for I was orphaned at an early age, and Max provided my keep and paid for my education. So I agreed to his plan—"

"—which involved nothing less than pretending to love me," Dramocles said bitterly.

"That part was not pretense," said Chemise. "I have loved you since I was a little girl. My scrapbooks were filled with your pictures, and I used to beg my uncle to tell me about you. It was my love for you that let me fall in with his terrible scheme. For, no matter what the outcome, I knew it would give me a chance to be near you for a while."

Dramocles lighted a cigarette and cried out, "Max, that damnable knave! What did he think he was playing at? I'll have his head for this!"

"Be not so hard on him, Lord. Oftentimes he spoke to me of the cruelty of his fate, condemned to deceive the man he most admired in the world."

"But who condemned him to it?"

"I do not know, Lord. You must ask Max."

Dramocles searched the asteroid, but he found that

his PR man had fled, stealing a spaceship and going to seek sanctuary among the barbarians of Vanir. Dramocles sat and considered, chain-smoking. At last he came to a conclusion. He knew where the final explanation had to lie. He ordered his ship prepared at once.

Dramocles' computer, dressed as usual in black cloak, white periwig, and embroidered Chinese slippers, was alone in its chambers at Ultragnolle Castle. It looked up when Dramocles entered.

"Home so soon from the celebration, my Lord?"

"So it would seem."

"And was it enjoyable?"

"Enlightening, let us say."

"There is an ambiguous edge to your words, Sire. Might something be distressing you?"

"Well," Dramocles said, "I suppose that I *am* a trifle put out by my recent discovery that, ever since Clara's arrival at court with that damnable clue to my destiny, my life has been influenced, nay, directed, by a mysterious backstage presence of uncertain intent."

"But you've known that, Sire. You refer, I presume, to the machinations of Otho the Weird."

"No. I am convinced that, whoever Otho was, he was directed by another."

"But who could that be?"

"Who but yourself, my clever mechanical friend?"

The computer adjusted its periwig with slow deliberateness, as though seeking a few moments' time in which to collect its thoughts. The gesture was purely theatrical, however, a deliberate attempt to act "manlike." The computer had long anticipated this moment and known what its response would be.

198

"How do you infer this, my Lord?"

"Simple enough," said Dramocles. "You are the greatest intellect on Glorm or Earth. You are also sworn to serve me. Therefore if the scheme against me had been of someone else's making, you would have warned me against it."

"Neat," said the computer. "Not foolproof, but very neat indeed."

"Do you deny my contention?"

"Not at all. You are perfectly correct, my King. Who else could have arranged these complex and arcane matters but I, Sir Isaac Newton's friend and your humble servant? I'm only surprised that you didn't consider the possibility earlier. But as the Taoists say, the sage passes unnoticed among the ranks of men."

"Damnation!" Dramocles cried. "I ought to get my tool kit and take you apart!"

"A simple command to disassemble would be sufficient," said the computer.

That statement quenched the King's fury. "Oh, computer," he cried, "why did you do it?"

"I had my reasons," the computer said.

"No doubt," said Dramocles, struggling not to get angry again. "May I hear them now?"

"Yes, Lord. You see, you are still missing one vital clue. It is the final mnemonic, and it will unlock the last of your suppressed memories. Then everything will be clear, and you will understand why certain matters could not be revealed to you before now. Shall I give you the clue, Sire?"

"Oh, hell, no, don't bother," Dramocles said. "I'm having too much fun playing dialectic with you. . . . Idiot, give it to me at once!"

The computer reached into a pocket within its cloak, took out an envelope, and handed it to the King.

Dramocles opened it. Within, there was a slip of paper.

Written on it were the words *Electronificate parsley*.

The last mnemonic! Deep in the recesses of Dramocles' mind, an unsuspected door swung open.

Twenty years old, ruler of an entire planet, the cynosure of all eyes and the repository of all hopes, young Dramocles was bored. King for less than a year, he was already sated with everything available to him. Dramocles wanted what he could not have—war, intrigue, love, hate, destiny, and, above all, surprise. But those were the very things that could not be. A fragile and uncertain peace existed among the Local Planets. To maintain it, a ruler of Glorm had to be judicious, peaceable, hardworking, predictable, devoted to precedent and procedure, holding court regularly so that his chamberlain could dispense justice according to the laws of Otho and his predecessors. To vary from this, to be unorthodox, or worse, *unpredictable*, could have unknown consequences, could even lead to war. Dramocles knew his duty. He was not going to risk the lives of millions for his amusement's sake, no, not even for his necessity's sake. He would go on, reasonably, sanely, *predictably*, until he toppled into his grave at last, Good King Dramocles, who wasted his life for the sake of his people.

Dramocles accepted his destiny, but found it bitter. Everyone else could hope for a change for the better; only the King had to wish for no change at all. In his unhappiness, he went to his computer.

200

The computer told Dramocles what he had already known—that he had to go on just as he was doing for the present.

"But how long will the present last?"

The computer made calculations. "Thirty years, my Lord. After that, you'll be free to do as you please."

"Thirty years? That's a lifetime! No. I shall abdicate, go away under an assumed name—"

"Wait, Sire—there's hope indeed. Do your kingly duty, and in thirty years I'll arrange for you to have all the things you really want. And you'll have time in which to enjoy them, too."

"How can you do that?" Dramocles asked.

"I have my ways," the computer said. "I am probably the finest intellect in the universe, I know you better than anyone, and I am your servant. Trust me to make your dreams come true."

"Well, all right," Dramocles said, a little ungraciously. "At least I'll have something to look forward to."

"I'm afraid not, Sire. Before I can begin, I must erase all knowledge of this from your memory. Your knowing that I was planning a future for you would add an incalculable input to your behavior, skew your reactions, and alter or render impossible the events I'm planning for you. It's called an Indeterminacy Situation."

"If you say so," Dramocles said. "But it makes me feel a little strange, knowing that I'll never remember this conversation."

"At the end," the computer promised, "you will get back all your missing memories, including this one."

Dramocles nodded. And then he was back in present time.

"What about Otho?" Dramocles asked. "What about Tlaloc?"

"My Lord," the computer said, "I can explain all the apparent discrepancies in the story. But do you understand the special terminology of the theory of provisional reality frames?"

"Never mind," Dramocles said. "I must admit, you went to considerable lengths to complicate my life."

"Of course, Sire. I acted on your behalf in producing this drama, and to the best of my ability gave you what you wanted. Love, war, family rivalry, intrigue, and a touch of mystery—all fine themes, all fit for a king. I wove these together into your destiny. But when I say that I did this, I mean that you did this, since you ordered me to program myself so that I could translate your dreams into reality. You yourself, my King, have been the shadowy backstage presence, the unknown figure who influences or directs your every move, your own secret prime mover."

"In that case," Dramocles said, "I suppose I should thank myself for all this. But you did well, too, computer."

"Thank you, Sire."

"Is there anything else left to tell?"

"Only this. Now I step out of the drama of your life. You go on, as free as a man can be, and that's a lot. It's all up to you now, Dramocles, to bungle your life as you see fit."

"You'll do anything to get the last word, won't you?" Dramocles said.

"Anything," said the computer.

"What do you know about my future?"

"Nothing, my Lord. It is unknowable."

202

"You're not kidding me, are you?"

"No, Sire. All is revealed, and I am going to take myself out of circuit shortly after we finish this conversation."

"You don't have to go that far," Dramocles said. "I was just wondering if you had anything else up your sleeve or down your circuits. 'Unknowable.' That sounds good to me." He left the room, rubbing his hands together briskly.

Filled with mathematical analogues for admiration and liking, the computer watched Dramocles go. The computer liked the King, to the small but significant degree that was available to it. Because of this, it was with a faint analogue of regret that the computer completed the last part of its program. It set forth certain impulses and got a response deep within its circuitry.

"Well done, computer."

"Thank you, King Otho."

"He doesn't suspect that there's any more than you told him?"

"I think not. Your son believes that he understands the laws of reality."

"And so he does, up to a point," said Otho. "We've done a good job with him, haven't we, computer? I love to see him enjoy the illusion of self-determination while I work behind the scenes to make sure his life works right."

"That's one way of looking at it, Sire. But perhaps you only have the illusion that you run your son's life."

"Eh?" Otho said sharply.

"The complications run deep," said the computer. "Each answer only brings us to another mystery. Sire, you played but a part in the drama you thought you were directing. And not too important a part, I regret to tell you. But now it is over. Good-bye forever, old King. Dramocles is just about as free as he thinks he is."

The computer realized that its last line was rather neat, so it decided to leave it at that. It was time to get offstage. Neatly, wildly, exquisitely, the computer shut itself down.